The A
of

A Spiritual Journey to Connect with the Universe and Discover your Life's Purpose

SHALINI BOOLUCK

Dear Ruchi,

I hope that you enjoy reading the novel.

Much love,

Shalini

ISBN-13: 978-1-3999-2936-3

Dedication

Dedicated to those who have lost hope,

And all of you, in search for love.

Don't underestimate the power of your own heart.

It will always show you the way.

God, grant me the serenity to accept the things I cannot change,

Courage to change the things I can,

And wisdom to know the difference.

The Serenity Prayer
Reinhold Niebuhr

As most of the action in the book takes place in India, the glossary at the back will help you with some of the unfamiliar vocabulary.

Table of Contents

Prologue

As Prana stared out at the ghostly silhouette of the London Eye from her balcony on floor 30, she could hardly breathe. She pushed a strand of her shiny ebony hair from her tanned face and tied it all in a long ponytail. She felt nauseous as she held on to the banister and stared at the tiny figures on the street.

"I give up," she whispered. Her dark brown eyes lost their glow as tears welled in.

She wondered what it would be like if she jumped from this luxurious apartment building. It would probably scare the hell out of old Tony who had suffered two mild heart attacks in the past. She could not have another attack of the security guy on her conscience. Assuming that she still has a conscience after death. Tony should not have to suffer for her problems. Still, she could not help picturing her slim tall body on the dark concrete below, her sleeveless pink dress and light brown skin covered in blood. It was not attractive. She was used to appreciative stares from men and at times envious ones from women, so it would be a shame to leave this world with the opposite effect.

Also, it would be unfair to create more stress for the people around. Londoners in the area were already quite stressed as it was. Someone would have to call an ambulance and the police. There would be a fuss for an hour, perhaps two, and then she would just be a forgotten body in a hospital morgue waiting to be flown back. This option was getting less tempting as her imagination got carried away. After doing her 360 degrees thinking about all options, Prana slowly let go of her grip on the banister. She decided to stick to her original plan.

She should never have trusted James. And now all that was left was this raging fire in her chest. It was the first time she had loved. A foolish mistake. She felt lost in this foreign country and longed to return to her paradise island, but it was too late now. The door to home had slammed shut the moment the plane left Mauritius. Her dreams of having a good job, a loving husband and two beautiful children will never become true.

Light drops of rain on her face brought Prana back to reality. She moved away from the edge of the balcony and went inside. She would see it through. She sat on the couch and reached out for the sealed box of sleeping pills from the coffee table. She felt submissive yet strong when she tore it open. As she felt the smooth texture of the tic-tac sized pills in the palm of her hand, a shadow of a doubt crept upon her but quickly vanished. She swallowed them one by one with what was left in her glass of red wine, enjoying the combination of excitement and apprehension building up in her chest. Here she was at 24, feeling in control of her life for the first time. It was her choice to die.

Within minutes, her mind and body relaxed. Her eyelids went heavy and everything around the living room started to look blurry. In that blissful space, pain ceased to exist. Both in her mind and in her heart.

She was floating. Did her body leave her? Or did she leave it? It did not matter. In this precise moment, everything was perfect just as it was. She was going to what so many people called Home.

She collapsed as a golden light embraced her.

She rested in that warm cocoon, finding peace at last.

Because you are alive,
Everything is possible.

Thích Nhất Hạnh

Chapter 1

When Death Rejects You, Aruna Retreat Welcomes You

India was a culture shock from the moment she landed in Delhi. Summer was supposedly coming to an end, but the stifling heat and humidity were relentless, the smell of human and animal excrement was sickening. The sky was dull grey from pollution. Prana's head felt heavy from all the noise and the heat made her irritable. Her silky hair now felt thick from the wet dust. The poverty affected her most. It tore her heart to see skinny children begging for food. As soon as she stepped out of the travel agency, five of them rushed towards her and pulled on her kurta with dirty little fingers. She did not understand their language, but the pain was clear in their begging eyes. Pain is the same whichever language you speak. The taxi driver who dropped her at the agency earlier had advised her not to give anything as, at the end of the day, the money would be taken away from the kids anyway. Two middle-aged men dropped the children there at 5a.m. every morning and picked them up in the evening. They took the money and in exchange fed them dinner and let them sleep on the porch, at the back of their house. If they were in a good mood, they might give them a glass of milk in the morning. The kids would be in trouble if they used the money. They had to beg for their lunch.

'*Why did I choose this place?*' Prana asked herself, as she hurried away. She had only been there a day but felt worse than in London. She started to regret not accepting Smita's offer to stay longer, but she did not want to take advantage of her friend's kindness. Smita had done a lot for her already from the moment she picked her up from hospital last week. Besides, Prana was getting claustrophobic in the one-bedroom flat. She hardly went out, for fear of bumping into James. She was relieved when she spotted a Starbucks. She ordered herself a tall, iced café latte and sat at the last available table by a window. A wave of nostalgia came over her as the coffee scent brought back memories of the first time she met James in a coffee shop. She had been good at blocking him from her thoughts until the aroma caught her off guard.

The loud beeping of a bus trying to overtake another one made her jump. She looked out and saw a brown cow spying on her a few inches from the window. She chose to ignore it and sipped her coffee. *'Here I am in this crazy country, surrounded with mad people and mad animals.'* The heaviness in her heart seemed an intrinsic part of her now. She was about to instinctively reach for her phone from her bag when she remembered having left it behind. She did not want to give in to the temptation of getting in touch with James again, or even worse, hoping every second that he would ring. Instead, she pulled the train ticket from her bag to double check that she would really be leaving Delhi the next morning. The lady at the travel agency had reassured her that Rishikesh was a good destination with a more pleasant climate and interesting sightseeing places.

Apparently, the sky was blue there, but she would have to see it with her own eyes to believe it. She felt drawn to visit Rishikesh after reading about a highly recommended spiritual sanctuary, the Aruna retreat. It was also known for its architectural splendour. She was not particularly religious nor spiritual, but the photos she found during a Google search triggered her interest. After a week, she felt a genuine spark of hope. She could not quite explain it, but something from the photos felt familiar.

Prana left the Delhi hotel two hours earlier than planned. She was worried about missing the train. She headed to the nearby train station with her rolling suitcase and a huge shoulder bag filled with snacks and bottles of water to keep her going for the six-hour journey. Her body had been struggling with the local food. Everything was spicy, even tea had *masala*! The language barrier did not help when she tried explaining what she was looking for in the small shops. She wished she had not crossed off *hindi* from her choice of subjects at school. People were surprised when she did not understand them as she could easily pass for an Indian girl with her Asian looks, until she started talking with her strong Mauritian French accent. Her ancestors were from somewhere in West India, but she had too much going on in her mind to worry about what people thought right now. Her clothes were baggy as she had already lost weight from exhaustion, stress, and a poor diet. She made her way through New Delhi Railway station, looking for the platform for the train to Rishikesh.

The crowded platforms were chaotic and packed with travellers, porters carrying luggage in their hands and on their heads, more beggars, suitcases, bicycles, barking dogs and stacks of wooden boxes. People rushed out of the approaching trains even before they came to a final stop. She rapidly made her way through this pandemonium holding on tightly to her suitcase. The agent had warned her to be vigilant. Many porters were not genuine ones employed by the station's office, but merely thieves who would either run away with someone's luggage or ask for a huge tip before giving it back.

Her platform was at the far end of the station. There was a noticeable change in atmosphere in this quieter area reserved for first-class trains only with mostly well-to-do people around, in business suits and carrying laptop bags. Some were talking on their mobiles, others reading the newspaper. Two middle-aged women sat on a bench looking bored as they watched people going past. No bicycles. No boxes. No stray dogs. Prana was delighted to see her train was already there. *Rani*, the queen, was like a real one waiting majestically at the far end of a battlefield. No wonder the ticket had been more expensive than she expected. She stepped in her compartment and was straightaway greeted by the cool air-conditioning that tickled her skin. She dropped her suitcase and looked around. Her relief was overwhelming, like someone who had found water after a thirsty stay in a desert.

The compartment was large and clean. Two comfortable-looking dark blue cushioned sleeper berths faced each other with sufficient space underneath to store luggage. The windows were wide enough to offer a good view of the outside scenery. The sky-coloured curtains contributed to a serene look. It could have been mistaken for a hotel room if it was not for the noise and the chaos you could still see through the windows on the other side of the railway tracks. Her weary body relaxed as she sat on the berth. She knew deep inside that the real reason she had been unable to sleep was because she felt homesick and hoped that this trip would help.

She looked at the opposite berth and thought, '*I hope it will be someone nice.*'

She pulled out her newly bought book *The Alchemist*, but the exhaustion caught up with her. Prana dozed off for half an hour until the noise of the compartment door sliding open woke her up. A short white woman with a wide-brimmed straw hat poked her head in.

'Hello young lady, mind if I join you?' she said, stepping in straightaway.

Prana pushed herself up on the berth. 'Not at all, I was hoping for some company.'

'I'm Rose Wells,' said the lady in a strong British accent. Her handshake was surprisingly firm for her small frame.

Prana introduced herself.

'What a beautiful name! *Prana,* the life force energy,' said Rose.

Prana smiled. She liked her journey companion already. She observed Rose from the corner of her eyes. Rose wore a short-sleeved white cotton dress, long enough to brush against her ankles, a round ruby pendant with matching earrings and dark red flat sandals. As she took off her hat, Prana noticed her long silvery hair tied in a perfect knot. She was naturally pretty with a light suntan and no makeup. She was perhaps in her fifties.

As she tucked her small suitcase away and made herself comfortable, Rose sighed. 'My poor feet can finally rest for a few hours!' Her voice was pleasant and smooth. 'Where are you from, Prana?'

'I was born and brought up in Mauritius, but I am currently studying in London.'

'You are very lucky! I have friends who have visited your island, and they said it is a breath-taking country.'

'It is one of the best holiday destinations,' replied Prana.

Rose opened a small bottle of sparkling water and drank it all in one go before saying, 'I hope to go there one day. We have a long journey ahead and I'd love to learn more about it.'

'You might learn so much that you will want to go there today itself!' Prana was pleased at the thought of not having to read a book. She had missed interesting conversations.

The stationmaster's whistle was loud and clear. There was a sudden jerk as *Rani* slowly eased out of the station. The rumble got louder as the train picked up speed and chugged its way out towards the rural surroundings. On both sides there were small huts snuggling close to each other. Kids were waiting close to the tracks and waved as they went by. Prana waved back with a big smile, happy to be on her journey. They were soon in the countryside heading south with landscapes of mustard fields. The lushness of the scenery was such a contrast to polluted Delhi.

Rose rearranged her cushions, sat cross-legged, and gave Prana a motherly look, as if she was about to start a once upon a time fairy-tale.

'What brought you to India, dear girl?'

Prana had rehearsed her reply a few times already as she knew people she came across would want to know. 'I wanted to do something different for my holidays instead of going back home. I was always curious to find out more about my culture and spirituality. After a bit of research, I found a spiritual sanctuary located near the Ganges which seems the ideal place for me. How about you?'

'I live in Edinburgh, but I consider India to be my second home. I come here three times a year for some holistic work at the Aruna temple in Rishikesh. I recommend you visit the sanctuary if it is not already on your list of things to do.'

'Aruna is my destination! I read about a well-known spiritual master there who guides people to find their purpose in life.'

Rose smiled warmly. 'Indeed, and there is a lot more. Various spiritual and sight-seeing activities are organised. Are you attending one of the summer retreats?'

Prana felt she could trust her. 'I signed up for the ten-day *Finding your Path* retreats.'

'That's a good choice. I facilitate a few sessions in this one. Some people come for two-day meditation workshops, others come for spiritual talks, but *Finding your Path* is more profound. It challenges who you think you are, until you find the true answer,' Rose's voice trailed off. 'Each participant has a different experience. Are you in search of your life path then?'

'I want to find peace.'

The words came out unexpectedly. It had not occurred to Prana that it was such a simple thing she wanted until now, but it was true.

Rose's eyes filled with compassion. 'This was also my prayer when I first went to Aruna fifteen years ago.'

Prana bent forward and asked hopefully, 'Did you find it?'

'Yes, dear girl.'

'Did it take long?'

'Only as long as I allowed it to take.'

'What do you mean?'

'I realised one day that peace had always been within me. I couldn't feel it previously as it was hidden by other emotions to which I had given priority.'

'I see,' said Prana, unsure what she meant but she did not want to be too nosy. 'Is your family there as well?'

Rose opened another bottle of water and drank it slowly. 'No, I came after I lost my husband and young daughter in a car crash. I was the one driving. I woke up every morning very angry about why I was the only one who survived. My experience in Aruna changed my life. I've learnt to accept what I cannot change. After all, blaming the Universe or myself was not going to bring them back. I still miss them, but there is also a deeper peace within me now. I can tap into it anytime.'

Her voice was so gentle that Prana could feel the peace.

'There was a reason why I survived. I discovered with time that my purpose in life was to help others cope with their loss, regret, guilt and much more. I used to be a businesswoman, always taken up by work and I hardly spared time for my family. I only realised how precious they were when I lost them. Often, we wait until it's too late to make changes.'

Prana felt the tears stinging her eyes. Her fingers trembled as she pulled a pack of tissues from her bag. '*Here I am, fed up of living while other people lose their loved ones too soon,*' she thought. Crying had become second nature. The more she tried to stop, the worse it got.

Rose bent forward and placed her hand on Prana's shoulder. 'Don't worry, sadness is a temporary emotion. Aruna is the right place to help you connect with your inner peace.'

Prana felt awkward. Rose was probably regretting sharing a compartment with her. 'I'm sorry. The past week has been very stressful for me and I'm not good at coping with pressure.'

Rose said nothing, only rested back against the soft cushions. The silence brimmed with unspoken words. Prana knew that she was being given the opportunity to say more, but she hesitated. She thought that Rose, who had been through a lot worse, might find her weak. She was not ready.

'Do you work in Edinburgh?' she asked.

'I have a private practice in town where I do the same therapy work as in Rishikesh, Reiki and Hypnotherapy. I've found the perfect balance in life, doing what I'm passionate about, in two countries that I love.'

'You are lucky. I hope to find my passion one day,' said Prana.

'It's such a rewarding feeling to see someone who's been feeling low find happiness again,' added Rose. 'Why are you sad Prana?'

Her straightforward question took Prana by surprise. She buried her face in her hands as fresh tears came up. She was not used to people showing compassion towards her. The pain in her heart began to melt. Perhaps there was no harm in opening up to a stranger.

'My relationship broke up last week. I feel so lonely. I don't know what to do, or where to go.'

'I hear despair in your words, but I see strength in your eyes. There's a reason to everything that happens even if it's not obvious at first. Aruna is a sanctuary where your broken heart will start to heal. Was he your first love?'

Prana looked up. 'How did you guess?'

'It's written all over your face,' said Rose affectionately.

'I had one boyfriend in high school, but nothing serious. James was my first love, and probably the last one.'

'Well, you are the only one in charge of your emotions. Your heart will follow the direction in which your thoughts take it. Give yourself time to heal.'

Prana felt slightly better already. Rose's voice had a calming effect on her.

'I wish I could go back in time and erase everything that happened in London,' she replied.

Rose shook her head from side to side. 'Relationships are the biggest gifts that offer us the opportunity to learn life lessons. You cannot change the past, but it is your choice whether to carry sad memories with you or let them go. The more you think about them, the harder it will be to forget.'

'It's not that simple …' Prana let her words drift away.

'If this is what you think, so it will stay. But you can also see an opportunity to discover where your strength comes from, and how to use it for finding true love.'

'I will not be able to love someone else.'

'Who said it has to be someone else?' said Rose softly. 'Start by loving yourself. Then see what happens naturally. Once you realise that you are worthy of love Prana, anything is possible again. Your dream of finding peace will turn to reality.'

'I will try,' murmured Prana, looking out of the window. Any form of love felt too painful right now. She could not face it. There was a noticeable change outside. White clouds spread across the pale blue sky like fluffy clumps of cotton-ball. The endless mustard fields were covered in yellow flowers. Occasionally, there would be some open huts where baskets and harvesting tools were kept. Small brownish brick houses, mostly hidden by the plants, were just about visible in the far background.

*****

'*Aap kuch khayenge?*'

Prana turned her head and screamed in panic when she saw a pair of pitch-black eyes staring at her, inches away from her face. The man's dark brown skin glowed from the beads of sweat that rolled down his face and arms. His chest was hidden behind an enormous box that was strapped to his neck and filled to the brim with all sorts of snacks and drinks. He looked like a gloomy ghost who had come back from the land of the dead, if such a thing was possible.

The old man pulled back, looking even more scared than them. *'Mujhe maaf karo. Mein khana bechta houn. Aap kuch khayenge?'*

Rose turned to Prana. 'Relax, he is just a food vendor.'

'I thought that they did not have access to the first-class section. Is it not meant to be safe here?' replied Prana, in a shaky voice.

'When trains stop at stations, they get in a low-class compartment at the other end and make their way through compartments. He looks like a good man, though.' Rose nodded in the direction of the man.

Prana felt sorry as she looked at him more closely. The man was skinny and perhaps in his sixties. He looked pitiable, on the verge of passing out from tiredness. His back arched under the weight of the heavy box. The skin on his bald head was peeling, probably from being exposed to the blazing sunshine, and revealed fat blisters about to burst with pus. The skin around his neck had flaked and the strap dug deep into the skin that looked painfully pink. He smelled of rotten eggs.

Prana looked away, feeling sick. She reached out for her bag and took some change from her purse to buy some water. She pointed to the bottles in the vendor's box and indicated with her fingers that she wanted three although she had enough to last her for the whole trip. She hoped that it would make the box light enough to relieve the man's back from the extra weight.

'Good idea. I'll buy some too,' said Rose.

The vendor happily handed them the bottles. His teeth shone as white as snow, and contrasted with his dark skin, when they told him that he could keep the change.

'*Dhanyavad! Dhanyavad!*' he said.

'You probably guessed. It means *thank you*,' said Rose.

He turned to leave, stopped after a few steps and walked back. He took a pack of crisps from the box and handed it to Prana. '*Yeh tofa aap ke liye kiunki meine apko dard kiya hain.*'

Rose smiled, 'He is saying this is a gift to apologise for upsetting you.'

Prana was irritated that the man was taking so long to go. She reached out to grab the pack of crisps and inadvertently looked into his eyes. This time what she saw was different and she could not look away. His eyes were filled with honesty and integrity. Suddenly, the blisters filled with pus, the flaking skin and the smell of rotten eggs were meaningless. She felt ashamed for judging this poor man who was doing what he could to earn his living honestly. A pack of crisps was probably cheap, but every cent made a difference in this man's life, and he was giving it to her for free.

'I'd like to know more about him. Would it be rude to ask?', checked Prana.

'On the contrary, he will take it as a compliment that you are acknowledging his presence. People like him are at times treated like stray dogs, who go around unseen,' said Rose.

'Could you please ask him if he has a family?'

The man gave them a broad smile when Rose asked him in Hindi. He looked younger and his exhausted eyes suddenly shone like tiny stars. His voice was filled with excitement.

'He has five children,' translated Rose. 'The eldest is 10 years old and works as a cleaner in a market. His wife stays in their hut most of the time to look after the other children, clean and cook.'

The man carried on passionately, like a car which started up after its dead battery had been recharged.

'On a lucky day, together with his son, they earn fifteen rupees. There are days when it's less than ten, but he still wakes up every morning feeling happy to have a family which is his reason to live. When he gets home at the end of a busy day and looks at them, he forgets his tiredness.'

Prana was shocked to learn that he was only 40. She smiled at him. He joined his hands together and bowed. She wasn't sure what it meant but she did the same when she saw Rose doing it.

The man left, humming joyfully.

'What does this gesture mean?'

'It's a *namaste*, an ancient Sanskrit sign of respect in India. It means *the divine in me bows to the divine in you*. It's often used both as a sign of greeting and farewell.'

'I don't know why, but I feel different after meeting this man.'

'India is the land of the divine. Now that you've embarked on a new journey to find peace, tests come and throw you off balance. You will find weeds where you expect flowers and flowers where you expect weeds.'

'Huh … can you say that again in simple words?'

'Your mind probably judged this man on his poor appearance at first, but you only truly saw him when you looked beyond, and your soul found his soul.'

Prana's cheeks went red as she thought, '*How does she do that, she keeps reading me like an open book!*' It didn't matter though as she was starting to feel close to Rose.

'You will meet more people like him who feel blessed despite leading a poor life. You can find richness in the eyes of a poor man and poverty in the eyes of a rich man. Some are covered in expensive jewels and outfits, have more money than they need, but they are depressed. Their life is deprived of happiness. They haven't found the diamond within themselves.'

'What diamond?' asked Prana.

'Their true self. It is only when we realise that our happiness emanates from within that we can make it last. If we associate happiness solely with other people or expensive gadgets, we are bound to feel sad again when we lose them.'

Prana enjoyed Rose's company. 'Are you one of the spiritual masters at Aruna?'

'No honey, there is only Master at the place. I am only a teacher who assists with the work,' replied Rose as she let her hair down and rested her head against a cushion. 'Our master is Aryaji. There is something special about him that makes him stand out from the crowd. His approach can be sharp or gentle, provoking or encouraging, serious or funny. Either you like him, or you don't.'

'Tell me more about him, please,' said Prana with curiosity.

'Although people call him ji, which means sir, he is a simple man of great wisdom. During *satsangs*, spiritual gatherings, he explains how to manifest our spiritual awakening by connecting with the universal wisdom and energy called Grace. We all share the same Grace, but we don't experience it at the same time as our paths are different. Think of it as a snake and ladder game. We all have the same destination at the top of the board, but we get knocked back or can move faster on our path, depending on our moves.'

'Is it when we find Grace that we find peace?'

'Grace is peace. When you let go of past stories and future expectations, you create space to connect with your inner wisdom and find lasting peace. Aryaji explains how challenges show up, at times when you least expect, to test your strength. They might leave you upset, depressed, angry, or scared but you can tap into Grace, anytime and anywhere.'

'This sounds a bit complicated for me,' said Prana, confused. 'Peace is the absence of trouble. Why do we have to go through so much trouble to get there?'

Rose threw her head back in laughter. 'It is always a challenging journey for something worthwhile. Although it might sound like pushing a boulder uphill, during the retreat you will learn to develop the necessary resources to find peace.'

After a moment of hesitation, Prana said, 'I will be totally honest with you. I dropped out of my course last week. Even if I miraculously find peace at the retreat, I don't know what to do afterwards. I have nowhere to go.'

'How about going back to your family in Mauritius?' asked Rose.

'I don't think it's the right time,' said Prana.

'Don't stress about it right now,' reassured Rose. 'You are making it harder for yourself if you think negatively even before taking the next step. Take it one step at a time. Where you have to go will reveal itself effortlessly as your life purpose gets clearer in the coming days.'

'How long will it take?'

'As long as you need. There will be moments of self-reflection when you spend time on your own and do mindfulness exercises. It will all make sense as the pieces come together during the course. But right now, you look exhausted dear girl. We still have a few hours of journey ahead. Why don't you have a rest?' suggested Rose.

Prana was asleep within minutes.

The secret of health for both mind and body is not to mourn for the past,
worry about the future, or anticipate troubles,
but to live in the present moment wisely and earnestly.

Paramahansa Yogananda

Chapter 2

Burning Back to Life *Satsang*

The magnificence of the Aruna temple exceeded her expectations. The photos posted on the website had not done justice to the place. The tall wooden gateways were delicately carved and painted with colourful images of a young Lord Krishna surrounded by gorgeous cow-herding girls known as *gopis* and white cows in the background. A stunning lotus-shaped temple made of white marble was built in the centre of the compound. It had 27 petals formed in clusters of three. The vastness of 30 acres of surrounding green landscape brought out the whiteness even more. Next to the temple was a lifelike statue of a light brown cow feeding its calf. As they walked closer, Prana counted eight statues of Krishna starting from his childhood and at the different stages of his life from a teenager until he was with the beautiful Radha, his beloved.

Devotees were praying and placed fruits and flowers in front of the statues. Some walked around the statues in circles while rotating lit incense sticks, before sticking them in ripe bananas to make them stand straight. Something was strange. Prana looked around, trying to figure out what it was. As she was about to ask Rose, she got it. It was the silence. '*I couldn't imagine anywhere as quiet in the whole of India,*' she thought. She had visited a chaotic temple in Delhi where people were pushing each other to stand in front of the biggest statue and get the offerings from the priest. Here, they queued up and waited for their turns. There were no priests, just the devotees doing their own rituals peacefully.

'Let's check in at the residents' house,' said Rose as she pointed towards the back of the temple.

They loaded their suitcases on a small vehicle that looked like a golf cart and Rose asked the driver to drop these at the residence while they chose the ten-minute walk to the place. They went through a square-shaped garden filled with a variety of roses and lilies to the left, and yellow marigolds and sunflowers to the right. The centre was decorated with a pond full of small white lotuses. There were patches of coriander, tulsi and mint herbs at the end.

Prana felt relaxed and happy to be stretching her legs after the long hours on the train. The sun was still at its peak, but the surroundings were so relaxing that it did not bother her anymore.

'Is it forbidden to talk near the temple?' she asked.

'It's only inside the temple when people are meditating, that silence should be respected. At times visitors choose to remain quiet outdoors as they want to preserve the stillness that they've experienced indoors.'

A cottage was situated at the entrance of the gate that led to the accommodation. A thick thatched roof rested beautifully on dark wooden walls, protecting the building from the heat. The wooden name sign *Crystal* carved in was swaying above the open doors. Shawls, kurtis and cotton trousers in patterned colours were displayed on hangers nailed to posts on the porch. As they walked past, Prana saw crystals and deity statues displayed on wooden shelves. Soft music was playing inside. She made a mental note to visit the place. The idea of treating herself to some new clothes was appealing.

The three-storey residents' house was simple-looking, with only ten rooms on each floor. It was welcoming even from outside. Each room had a small balcony with a few flowerpots and a rocking chair. The old reddish bricks brought warmth to the place. The sun had left its imprint through the noticeable cracks in some bricks.

'Don't worry, this building has been here for over a century and it's strong enough to welcome many more generations,' said Rose.

'I love this place already,' replied Prana with a smile. 'I plan to find peace and discover my life purpose here.'

'What a good start. The magic of Aruna is working already!'

The lady in the small lobby seemed to be expecting them.

'Welcome, I am Rupa. It's lovely to see you again Rose,' she greeted them from behind the desk. 'And you must be Prana?' she said, turning to her.

Prana nodded.

'You are both on the first floor. Your luggage is upstairs already.'

She handed them their bedroom keys and a form for Prana to fill in.

Rose thanked her and turned to Prana, 'I'll let you carry on with the registration. Now is a good time to recharge our batteries. Have a good rest dear girl.'

She hugged Prana before making her way towards the staircase.

Soon after, Prana handed her details back to Rupa and headed upstairs to room 17. It was like being in a college hostel. The first thought that came to her as she opened the bedroom door was, '*God help me!*'

She had forgotten all about the luxuries she had back home until now. The butterfly wallpaper, vanity table and king-size bed all seemed to be from a faraway land. They belonged to the girl who used to enjoy a margarita while watching the sunset on a Mauritian beach, the one who used to drive her BMW with the air-conditioning on while listening to pop music. That girl did not exist anymore. In fact, she stopped existing the moment she moved to London, but it was only now that reality struck her like lightning.

The room was clean but bare. White walls, a single bed with a thin mattress, a small wardrobe, an old ceiling fan, a wooden table that fitted in a corner and a chair from which the fabric was coming off. A rolled-up yoga mat was resting against the wardrobe. The fresh lemony scent suggested that the room had been cleaned recently. There was an open door to the bathroom. The beige curtain was so thin that the light shone right through. '*Waking up early won't be an issue here*,' she thought. She enjoyed weekend lie-ins and she could tell that leisure was going to be rare in this place.

Prana picked up an activity leaflet from the table. Her eyes nearly popped out when she read the time on the first line. '*Yoga & Guided Meditation by Nathan, 7- 8 a.m.*' She felt a knot of apprehension in her stomach, but at least it did not say compulsory. Later during the day, Rose was responsible for *Emotional Progress* sessions. As she had a quick glance through the leaflet, she saw some interesting ones on Letting Go, Beliefs Change, Loving your Inner Child, Forgiveness and Life Purpose. Prana felt particularly drawn to the Letting Go and the Law of Attraction ones but knew already that she would probably attend all of them as Rose had already won her heart. There were strange activities like *Shakti Dance, Laughter Meditation* and *Walking Meditation*. She was sceptical about the meditation ones. '*How can we walk or laugh and meditate at the same time?*'

The leaflet also mentioned that residents were invited to explore the organic fields that belonged to the temple and join farmers in the harvesting. It was a simple way to connect to Mother Nature. Outings were organised to the Ganges. The satsangs were held every afternoon. Residents were encouraged to observe a daily 30-minute silence in the temple at any time of their choice, whether on their own or in a group. Prana folded the leaflet and put it in her bag. She was too tired right now to make sense of all the information. She understood better why Rose mentioned that some people left after a few days. Aruna was certainly not a holiday retreat. Rose said that people keen on progressing spiritually gathered here and Prana wanted to be one of them. Although her dreams had been shattered, she refused to spend the rest of her life crying over spilt milk.

After a short nap, she refreshed and got ready to explore the place before going to the satsang. She wore a new light green kurti with matching dark green leggings. She was shocked when she looked in the mirror. She had lost so much weight. The girl who stared back at her had black rings under her eyes and her skin was pale and dry. The thought of spending the rest of her life in such an appalling state was depressing. She hung a towel over the mirror to spare herself this eyesore again.

She walked barefoot as she made her way back to the temple, enjoying the sensation of the soft grass beneath her feet. She came across a few people who smiled at her as if they already knew each other. It was such a warm feeling to be around kind people. She forgot all about her pitiful state and felt a new warmth in her heart as she smiled back.

There were nine tree-shaped entrance doors to the temple, all made of white marble. She felt small as she walked in and looked up the 30 metres height to the ceiling. The temple was spacious with some long marble benches. The energy was vibrant inside. Rays of sunshine peeped in through the tall and narrow windows. A three-metre-tall amethyst crystal rested impressively in the centre. It was naturally carved and shone where rays of sunlight caressed it. The irregular carvings in several areas brought out the natural beauty of this masterpiece. A handful of people were sitting in silence. Some were meditating with open eyes, their full attention focused on the crystal. Prana joined them, and much to her surprise, she found the silence more intimidating than relaxing. She wanted to leave after a couple of minutes, but it was too late. Memories that she had been pushing away for weeks came back with a vengeance. She could hear James laughing, as if he was right here by her side, and she remembered the first time he swept her up in his arms and carried her to his bedroom. The warm sensation of his body on hers as they lay naked in bed, his hungry kisses, the feeling of urgency as they made love for the first time, the tears of pleasure… She shook her head, but in vain. The more she tried to push away the thoughts, the memories came flooding in even more.

She left the temple feeling utterly ashamed that such thoughts had surfaced in this sacred place.

****

The satsang room, situated next to the temple, was beautifully decorated. The walls held antique handmade paintings of the Hindu Gods and Goddesses. The dimmed lights gave a warm welcome to the place. The scent of sandalwood incense and a gentle instrumental music that played in the background were soothing. Several brass oil lamps were burning along the walls. The sitting area was divided into two sections with rows of five chairs on each side. Cosy cushions were kept in a corner for those who preferred taking one of them and sitting on the thick plum-coloured carpet. The place could comfortably hold fifty people. A small stage was raised at the far end with a beige sofa in the centre and a brass oil lamp burning on one side. A vase of snow-coloured roses, a glass of water and a microphone were placed on a low maple table on the other side. The paintings that hung on the wall behind illustrated a point of light in the centre with rays of lights spreading in all directions on an orange background.

The room was filling up quickly, with people from their early twenties to a few elderly ones in wheelchairs. Some were busting with energy, others looked fragile. There was a mixture of different origins with a mixture of expressions: excitement and anxiety, alertness and tiredness, happiness and fear, smiles, and tears. Some helpers dressed in simple white cotton kurtas were standing by the walls.

Prana took a seat in the third row next to a friendly looking young girl. Her anticipation was growing. She would finally meet Aryaji, the 50-year-old guru of universal spirituality. After her conversation with Rose, she hoped from the bottom of her heart that he would be able to help her. She had not seen any photos of Aryaji as he was known to be a humble man. He did not call himself a master; visitors started using this word and it became anchored with time.

The room fell silent when he walked in. His strong presence brought a natural sense of awareness. Prana turned her head and her jaw dropped when she saw him. He was far from what she had expected. She had imagined an ordinary-looking old priest with a white beard. Aryaji had striking features. His long nose perfectly matched his high cheekbones and strong jawlines. He was 6-foot tall with a slim figure and had a warm walnut complexion. His shoulder-length salt-and-pepper hair had a natural waviness that added to his relaxed demeanour. He wore an orange silk kurta and had a row of clear crystal beads around his neck. His overall appearance was sophisticated. Some people did a namaste as he made his way to the stage, spreading a peaceful energy on his way. His brown eyes held oceans of serenity. Prana felt waves of love and calmness embrace her as he walked past.

Aryaji sat cross-legged on the sofa and *namasted* as he looked around, taking a moment to rest his eyes on each person present. Prana felt her whole body go numb when he looked deep in her eyes. It felt like he was looking beyond her physical body, right to the heart of her soul and yet it didn't feel intrusive. She wished this moment would last a lifetime. She knew without a shadow of a doubt that she was in the right place. As he looked past her to the other guests, it felt like he had made a lifetime connection with her.

His voice floated out, pleasant and smooth as he held the microphone. 'Namaste, dear ones. Let us observe our usual one-minute silence before starting. You can close your eyes, or you may prefer to focus on the point of light in the poster behind me … choose what is easier for you.'

Prana was unable to focus on anything. She could hear the man behind her breathing in deeply and when he breathed out, the air tickled the back of her neck. The background noise of the fan was distracting. The lady next to her had sprayed a whole can of deodorant. '*It is unbelievable how we become more aware of what is going on around with closed eyes*,' she thought.

After what felt like an endless minute, Aryaji said, 'Take a nice deep breath in and let it out. You may now open your eyes. I would like to welcome the fifteen persons who have joined us today for the *Finding your Path* retreat. Satsang is a gathering where we work with the power of Truth. It brings up to the surface whatever has been blocking you from discovering the journey to your own self. Strong emotions, that you might not even have felt previously, might come up like a volcano in eruption.'

'For some of you, it might be a short journey where meditations are enough as your volcano is dormant and remains this way. This is fine also. You will go back to your daily life feeling refreshed and you can meditate daily to preserve this peaceful state. You don't need to force anything to happen. For those of you who came here as seekers of a deeper experience, you have the opportunity to find an authentic connection with your inner self, your Truth. That is when you feel the eruption, a deeper twist taking place to your life. No matter how much you might want to carry on doing what you are in life, somehow life will always throw challenges your way. Things will go wrong, be it in relationships, work, or health. You will be guided to discover your life purpose elsewhere. This could be why you are here today.'

He reached out for his glass and took a sip of water. His fingers were long, and he wore a star-shaped ring with an amethyst stone in the centre on the index of his right hand. 'There is no right or wrong. Go with what feels right for you. If you don't know what it is, then don't do anything. Just wait and the answer will come your way. The first step is the same for everyone … letting go of memories. When we surrender to emotions that are stuck with old memories, and no matter how hard it feels at first, we start to see the light at the end of the tunnel. It is important to focus on the Now, what we call the *present moment awareness.* Once we accept what happened in the past, it makes it easier to move on. In today's satsang, we'll talk about how holding on to unhealthy memories affects our life. Who would like to share first?'

He had an encouraging smile, like a teacher looking at his students. 'Perhaps a childhood trauma, a heartbreak or a health problem that started when you were going through a rough phase?'

Silence.

'Or we can all just hang out together in silence,' he chuckled. This was enough to break the ice as some people started laughing.

A man in his early forties raised his hand and one of the helpers brought him a microphone. He stood up slowly and held on to the chair in front of him to keep his balance. He had a thick cotton scarf wrapped around his neck. His face was wrinkled in pain as he spoke. 'I am Jayan. Six months ago, I was diagnosed with polyps. At my doctor's advice, I have been talking as little as possible but when I had another laryngoscopy last week, the number of polyps had doubled and grown bigger. I am not troubled by memories. I don't know what is wrong.'

He paused to catch his breath. 'A friend told me that you are a great master and healing miracles can happen here. I wake up every day, worried that the benign polyps might become cancerous.' His tone was gripped with despair.

All eyes turned to Aryaji, waiting for his reply.

'Jayan, did you come because you believe from the bottom of your heart that you can heal? Or because others have healed after coming here?' asked Aryaji firmly.

The man's face changed in excruciating pain as he coughed. 'I want to heal. Please help me.'

'When I look at you, I see someone who has already accepted defeat. You need to trust that you can do it. We are here to provide you the extra support, but you have to put in your own determination and perseverance.'

Jayan waited for his dry coughing to pass and said, 'Trust? I pray daily, but God ignores me. I have always been an honest man who goes to work and takes care of his family. I never drank alcohol, nor smoke. I have done nothing to deserve such a punishment!'

'If it is not an obvious cause, let us look at other possibilities. Was there a big change in your life last year before you started the polyps?'

'Something significant happened but it did not affect me for long,' replied Jayan bitterly.

'How did you manage to get over it quickly when you still sound bitter talking about it today?'

'I blocked the memories away,' admitted Jayan.

'It is crucial to accept the memories and to face the pain they trigger. It becomes harmful over time if you bury them and pretend, they never happened. This is a dangerous game that you are playing,' said Aryaji.

Prana felt shivers going down her spine as she heard those words. Aryaji's expression was stern, and you could tell that there was no messing around with him. She felt tense thinking of her own memories that seemed to be always around.

Jayan's voice brought her back to the moment. 'Why should we face painful memories again? It feels like going backwards instead of making progress.'

'Suppressed memories can lead to suppressed unhealthy emotions. The common ones are anger, rage, fear, guilt, sadness, and resentment. Emotionally traumatic experiences can set up a trigger causing a toxic build up in the cells. Over time this causes dysfunction as the body's ability to maintain balance is blocked. However, the body never lies. Your mind might ignore the emotions, but they start to manifest in the body, and like a volcano, they erupt in the form of emotional or physical illnesses,' explained Aryaji.

Some people murmured in agreement.

'I guess it makes sense,' said Jayan.

Arja ji looked at him straight in the eyes. 'What happened last year? What if you could welcome the thoughts that you suppressed back then, once again.'

Jayan closed his eyes and took a deep breath. 'It is not easy, but I can see a part of it again. I found out last year that my wife of twenty years was cheating on me. The first thought that came to my mind was *What will people think?* I chose not to say anything to her in case she left me. I would not have been able to bear the humiliation.'

'Are there emotions you wished you had expressed back then?'

'Eventually, she left me. I kept quiet when she left me for this other man. I let her go without saying anything because I did not want to look pitiable. I can't tell you the number of times when I say to myself that maybe if I had swallowed my ego and tried to fix our marriage, we might still be together. You must be thinking what a coward I am …'

'It takes courage to open up and show your vulnerability,' said Aryaji gently. 'I'd like you to look around.'

When Jayan turned his head, he was blown away by the compassion and understanding in people's eyes.

Aryaji's voice resonated. 'There is no judgement here. We all have our own story and you have shown immense courage by sharing yours with us. This is real strength. Praying in a temple and waiting for a miracle to happen is not the solution.'

He turned to the group. 'Can you see the link between what happened to Jayan last year and the polyps? It is not always the case, but throat diseases can indicate swallowed anger. It is a wake-up call from the body to let go of the emotions that you wish you had expressed, but that you kept inside.'

'Jayan, here is a piece of homework for you. Make a list of things you wish you had said in the past but did not. This is not only about your wife, but anything that you can remember from childhood up to now. Once you get the thoughts out on paper, it becomes easier for the emotions to follow. We can then release these emotions that might be blocking your path to healing. We have special sessions to help.'

'Trust the Universe and yourself,' he added. 'You can turn your enemy into your best friend if you start using your mind to heal your body. Wake up every morning, convinced that you are better than yesterday. Positive intentions lead to your healing. If this is hard, you can look at it from a different perspective. Ask yourself, if you were to die tomorrow, what can you do to make the most of the time that you have left? The more you do it, the better you will feel. Ask this question every day.'

'I feel hopeful already,' replied Jayan with a hint of relief in his voice as he sat down.

Aryaji returned his attention to the group with a big smile. 'If any of you is going through something similar, I recommend you try the same exercise. Go back to childhood. The root cause to issues usually starts there. Our behavioural patterns and set trajectory are formed during childhood. They affect what we attract towards us as we grow older. When your list is ready, you can join Rose's session where she will take you through the process of letting go.'

He carried on, 'Most of you have come here for some sort of healing, for finding peace or for spiritual progress. It is important to clear past emotions that don't serve you, or else it is like moving up a mountain with a lead ball tied to your ankle. It is not only frustrating, but also impossible and even if you make it to the top, you will be too drained to enjoy the rewarding view.'

There were a few nods.

'Who else would like to share?' encouraged Aryaji.

Quite a few hands bravely came up this time, including Prana's, much to her own surprise.

She found it encouraging listening to Jayan's experience. She felt compassion for him, but also being reminded that there were people who suffered more than she did made her feel better. She was not proud of her thought but could not help it.

She felt a mixed freezing and melting sensation when Aryaji's eyes rested on her.

Jayan passed her the microphone.

Aryaji smiled warmly. 'Welcome, it's the first time I see you here.'

She stood, feeling a new strength that emerged from nowhere. His words felt like an electric jolt that sent shivers down her spine. 'My name is Prana.'

'Ah, the life force … is it your intention to awaken your *kundalini* energy?'

'If this can be done within ten days, why not…' replied Prana.

'Depending on how ready you are, it can take a second … or a lifetime. What brought you here?'

Prana's voice came out strong and even. 'First of all, I would like to say that I had a happy childhood. I was an only child, and my parents gave me everything that I needed. I can't see how what happened to me is connected to my past.'

'Everything doesn't necessarily go back to childhood,' explained Aryaji. 'But let us not put the cart before the horse and make assumptions before hearing your experience.'

Prana nodded. 'Recently, I went through a painful unexpected breakup. It hit me like a slap on the face. Nine months ago, I went to London to start a course at university. I was staying at the hostel. A few months later, I met James in a coffee shop, and it was love at first sight for both of us, or so I thought. We met almost every day and he called me every evening. After four months together, we thought that it would be a good idea to move in together. From that point on, our relationship changed abruptly. Last month was the worst part, something happened, and he asked me to leave.'

Tears welled in her eyes. 'I had nowhere to go. I didn't want to upset my parents, so I stayed with a friend before coming here. Since this happened, I've been feeling like I'm drowning in a pitch-black hole. Unlike Jayan here, for me memories keep coming up. When I think of the time I spent with James, I sink deeper into despair. I feel scared to death about what will happen next.'

'You are keeping yourself prisoner in this black hole,' said Aryaji kindly. 'Your thoughts are shaping your behaviour, which in turn create strong long-lasting memories. It seems to me that at a subconscious level, you don't want to move on because you haven't yet accepted what happened. You have the power to control your subconscious mind and you have the choice whether to remain stuck in the past or turn the page and create a positive future. Be careful which direction you choose. Death is a powerful word; don't give it control over life.'

Prana felt her heart explode with excruciating pain. 'What if death brings me everlasting peace?'

The atmosphere changed as Prana brought the elephant into the room. Her wish to die was unmistakable.

'Seeking one's own death is running away from the truth. True peace comes from accepting the worst. You cannot change what has happened Prana. The past is done. Surrender to it. Welcome memories when they come up. There is nothing to do. Simply watch them, like an old movie. Tune into what is within, this is where you will find peace. Then, let it go. Let the screen go off as you come back to the present time,' replied Aryaji.

Prana hesitated for a few seconds. 'How can I stay in the present when every day I am reminded that my life will never be the same again?'

'Because this is the truth. It will never be the same. Stop worrying about what will happen next. What if it could be even better? Have you even thought about that? I suggest that you take some time to meditate. When you still your mind, answers that you need will come naturally.'

'Embrace the pitch-black hole with love. It came here to guide you on your path to spiritual awakening. What you are looking for is in the core of this dark hole. It is not an easy path, but you have the power to transform this darkness into a lighthouse.'

'Thank you,' said Prana as she sat down.

Her heart was pounding. She was even more scared after this conversation. She could hear James's harsh words echoing inside her head again. She rubbed her forehead as she had a flash of him pushing her against the wall.

Now that she had opened Pandora's box, there was no going back.

*****

About forty people were in the dining area that evening. It was a simple looking room with white walls, a grey tiled floor, and matching thick stripy curtains. Magenta- and fuchsia-coloured abstract paintings on the walls gave the room a warm energy. Round tables that seated four were on the left side of the room, covered with light blue plastic sheets, and surrounded with dark blue plastic chairs. Two rows of tables and chairs were neatly aligned a couple of metres away with a sign showing '*Silence Please*' placed in front. This was for those who wished to eat while maintaining their silence space.

A mouth-watering aroma was rising from the buffet at the back. Prana had not realised how hungry she was until the flavour of Indian curry tickled her nostrils. She filled her plate with white rice, yellow *tarka dahl* and a generous portion of mixed vegetable curry before making her way to the tables. She was exhausted but did not want to be on her own after the intense satsang. She spotted the girl who had been sitting next to her earlier and joined her.

'Hi, I'm Emily from Malaysia,' said the young plump girl with her mouth full. Black curls with orange stripes surrounded her young face. Behind the red glasses frame that sat on her short nose bridge, her narrow eyes were hidden by the over-mascaraed lashes. The glossy wine lipstick matched her dress.

'Hi, I haven't felt this hungry in weeks,' said Prana as she joined her.

'All the food looks so delicious that I thought I'd try a bit of everything,' added Emily, sheepishly. Her plate was filled to the brim.

Prana liked her straightaway, perhaps because she stood out from everyone with her fancy looks, which made her like a breath of fresh air after the intense satsang.

'I can understand why. I found it difficult to choose what to go for myself,' she said. It did not take long for her to suss out that Emily was talkative.

'I arrived in India two weeks ago to attend a detox and cleanse programme at an Ayurveda centre. The programme was meant to make me shed off fifteen extra kilos, but sadly it wasn't very successful as I lost only one kilo. A lady at the centre told me that I might be luckier here at the ten-day retreat. She said that Aruna brings healthy changes in people's lives, both emotionally and physically.'

Prana nodded, aware that Emily was waiting for a sign from her before carrying on.

'I am not sure how this will work out for me if they provide such good food every day,' confessed Emily as she shifted uneasily in the chair that was too small for her. 'Thank you for sharing your experience earlier. It helped me feel better knowing that there are other people who go through worse.' She realised a bit late that it was a tactless comment and hastily said, 'Sorry, I did not mean to offend you!'

Prana glanced around to make sure no one else heard her. 'Don't worry, I felt the same when Jayan spoke before me.'

She started laughing and Emily joined in. They were soon chatting like old friends and did not notice Rose approaching. They both jumped when she spoke.

'I was hoping you ladies would find each other. I knew you would get along like a house on fire,' said Rose with a smile.

'I felt beaten up after satsang but now I'm a lot better,' said Prana.

'Excellent,' replied Rose. 'You are experiencing an energy release as you let go of some emotions after sharing. Today was only a warm-up. The coming days will be more intense.'

'I am not a spiritual seeker,' said Emily. 'I only want to lose weight.'

'Losing weight is a piece of the puzzle. If you have come all the way here, it is for more to it. Everything will slowly fall into place, like a jigsaw puzzle.'

'I see,' replied Emily while biting into a piece of potato.

From the look on her face, Prana could tell that she had not understood anything of what Rose meant. Neither had she.

'I suggest that you both have an early night. There will be more to process tomorrow. I wish you both a good night rest,' said Rose, before leaving in the direction of the bedrooms.

If we are creating ourselves all the time,
then it is never too late to begin creating the bodies we want
instead of the ones we mistakenly assume we are stuck with.

Deepak Chopra

Chapter 3

1st session – Freedom from a Lifetime of Garbage

The ambience in the conservatory was relaxing. '*No wonder it is called the Angel Room*,' thought Prana. She recognised a subtle fragrance of frangipani as she walked in. Chairs covered with soft patterned cushions were placed in a semi-circle in the middle of the room. There was a round wooden table at the centre, barely visible under plain paper sheets, pens, and a tissue box. A whiteboard was placed nearby, and thick yoga mats were spread on the floor for those who might need a rest. Gentle music was playing in the background.

Three people were already seating. She recognised Jayan and Emily. Jayan looked grey like a ghost, a real contrast next to Emily. He had a thick brown shawl wrapped around his throat, drooped shoulders and his eyes were lifeless. Emily was wearing a bright blue dress with an expensive looking pearl necklace, matching earrings, and black shiny high-heeled shoes. Her face was caked in make-up, but it did not spoil her bright smile.

The other man introduced himself as Dev. His shaved head was shining. His round face was partly hidden with a thick beard and a big curly moustache. Prana felt his warm and friendly energy as she sat next to him, and they shook hands.

Rose soon joined them and sat cross-legged on a small couch, with a cushion tucked behind her back. She looked serene in a canary yellow dress and her long hair hanging loose around her face. 'Namaste friends, you have already taken a big step by coming. Our *Letting Go* session requires willingness to bring up old pain and feel it again, maybe even stronger this time as other memories might come up with it. As Aryaji said, it is hard work. We need courage and perseverance.'

She looked at Prana and Jayan. 'Well done for sharing during satsang. We are all stronger than we realise. I have worked with hundreds of people. Each one's life experience is different, yet similar in some way.'

'How is this possible?' questioned Emily.

'We all have our own stories, but emotions are the same. It doesn't matter which country you are from, or what is your gender and religion, there is only one type of pain. Pain is pain. Love is love. Anger is anger. In today's session, we will learn how to stop engaging with the stories, they are only time wasters. The first step is to surrender to what is here,' explained Rose.

'As you all probably already know, we ask for guidance and wisdom from the Universe, God, the archangels, our guardian angels, or a higher spirit. Whoever you feel comfortable with.' She lit a tea-light candle that was placed in the centre of a rose quartz crystal holder before looking at Jayan. 'Have you done your homework?'

Jayan nodded as he pulled a piece of paper from his pocket. 'I was surprised to end up with a page full of the times when I did not express how I felt. Only half of those memories are connected to my wife, the rest are with other members of my family, friends and even colleagues.'

'Good work,' Rose looked at the others and said, 'We are all in this together. During Jayan's process, you can support him with love and compassion.'

Prana, Emily, and Dev nodded. They already felt close to him and respected him for sharing such personal information.

'Jayan, please close your eyes, sit up with your spine straight and focus on your breath,' said Rose softly. 'Visualise a wooden door in front of you. Walk towards it and open the door, there is a very special angel or God waiting for you.'

Jayan placed his hands on his knees. His body relaxed as he started to breathe deeply and slowly. 'I can see god Ganesh, the remover of obstacles.'

Rose encouraged him. 'Wonderful, and now ask Ganesh to take you on a trip inside your body, to your throat. Describe it when you reach this area.'

It did not take Jayan long to visualise as he prayed to Ganesh every day. 'It is sore and burning red like a hot oven. Hard lumps everywhere like tennis balls.'

'How does this make you feel?'

'Nervous and angry. I want to kick all those hard lumps out. They have invaded my territory!'

'Bring all the anger and nervous feelings to this present moment with us. Now, what is the earliest memory that comes back?' asked Rose.

Jayan's voice started shaking. 'My mum passed away when I was five. Some aunties comforted me, but no one explained why she left. They just said, *it was her time to leave.* Many times, I asked my father, but he did not show any sign of being affected. He told me that life goes on and I will get used to mum not being here. From that moment onwards, I learnt to hide my pain.'

He broke down in tears. Prana passed him some tissues.

'I was angry at him, at my mum, at my aunties, at the whole world for not explaining to me something that changed my whole life. I lost my mum's love, and I did not know why. When I had a nightmare, I would switch the light on and wait for her to come and comfort me. At times when I came back from school, I would go from one room to another, hoping to find her. Maybe she was playing hide and seek and forgot to come out?'

There was so much profoundness in his words that it felt as if the vulnerable little Jayan was coming back.

'Jayan, can you see how the anger trapped inside of you as a child spread in your body and took over, asking to be acknowledged? It manifested as an illness that cannot be ignored any longer. Were you in other relationships before meeting your wife?'

'I had one girlfriend when I was twenty.'

'What happened then?'

'She left me after two years. I don't know the exact reason, but I often thought she would leave me. She just said that it did not work for her.'

'Why didn't you ask her?' said Rose.

'It didn't matter. She had made her decision,' replied Jayan.

'Can you see the pattern that started from childhood when your mum left without explanation and how this anchored and repeated itself over time?' said Rose gently.

Jayan frowned, 'I don't understand.'

Rose explained, 'Your subconscious mind lived with the belief that women would always leave, just like your mum. As a child, you were not allowed to ask what was happening and you grew up with swallowed anger.'

She paused to let the words sink in. 'The quality of our thoughts determines the quality of what manifests in our life. You have been sending out a strong message to the Universe that women will always leave you and the Universe responded to your belief and anger, creating a pattern.'

Jayan looked shell-shocked, as if he had been struck by lightning. He groaned. 'I never would have thought—'

'An angry person is full of poison. Your poison is the unexpressed words and emotions stuck in your throat,' replied Rose. 'We found the root cause of the pattern that led to your illness, it is time let go of this unhealthy belief. They are thoughts that only waste your time. Stay with the emotion.'

'I hate my family even more now. It all happened because of them!'

'Stay with the anger. Allow it to become even stronger.'

Jayan started shaking violently with anger. His fists were clenched.

'Is there any emotion that feels even stronger than anger?'

'Deep rage,' shouted Jayan, oblivious to his throat pain.

'Burn in that rage. Nothing else exists,' said Rose firmly.

Suddenly, Jayan's face changed completely. Rose went to him and held him close as all the tears of the 5-year-old little boy started flowing. More tears came pouring out as memories of the boyfriend in him who was left came up, and the husband who was cheated on were unblocked.

'That's it, surrender and let go of the old stories completely.'

His body calmed down as the waves of tears subsided.

Rose pulled back slowly and asked, 'How are you feeling?'

'I feel an emptiness in my heart, but my throat is hurting so much. The polyps feel like poison.'

'Be gentle with your body,' said Rose. 'Let us clear the years of toxins. Visualise the throat scene again, with Ganesh and you standing there. Check with him how he can help to make it healthier.'

As Jayan concentrated, a tiny smile forming on his face. 'Ganesh is squirting water from his trunk on this whole part of my throat. I can see the red burning areas soothing down. The colour is starting to change to a lighter pink. It feels very sensitive and hurts. There are pink healing bubbles floating around.'

'Beautiful,' said Rose. 'What about the tennis ball polyps lumps?'

Jayan started laughing as he sat upright in his chair. 'They are turning into small marshmallows. It is taking time, but they are getting softer. Ganesh is picking them one by one with his trunk and they dissolve as he swallows them.'

'So now that the scene is turning to pink and the lumps are going, one by one, visualise a new image. How would you like it to look?'

'There is a waterfall. It keeps the area clean and pleasantly cold with fresh water. I can see myself as a little boy playing in the water with Ganesh. He is happy as he has a new friend with whom he can share how he feels. We go around with a wet cloth wiping the throat area so that it stays clean and healthy.'

'Great job, Jayan! What about the emptiness that you felt in the heart earlier?'

'Every day I travel down Ganesh's trunk to visit my heart area. I spend some time there as I watch angels filling the space with love and light. It takes some effort, but I also enjoy it.'

'Imagine your heart is an inner temple where love keeps growing. There is always space for more love.'

'My throat is throbbing with a combination of pain, excitement and immense relief.'

'Thank you for so much openness today,' replied Rose. 'This is what happens when we let go of stories and surrender to emotions. When you feel ready, you can gently open your eyes.'

Jayan's eyes were shining. They all hugged him.

Prana's eyes were red from tears and Emily had mascara all over her cheeks. Dev patted Jayan's shoulder before pulling two tissues from the box and wiping his own eyes.

Rose's voice floated softly. 'Look at one another.'

Prana looked at Dev first. She felt a wave of compassion when she saw the same in his eyes. It was the same when she looked at Emily and Jayan. She wanted to give them all a big hug. They understood each other without having to say a thing. A new bond had been created.

Rose waited a minute before adding, 'What you see in each other's eyes reflects you.'

Dev cleared his throat and said, 'Rose, I would not cry in front of my family. I don't understand how it happened so easily here. I don't feel like I have to hold it all together.'

'You answered your own question. You don't have to hold it all together. It is often easier to express how we feel with strangers as we are not worried about being judged or blamed. Often, we feel closer to strangers than family because we choose to create this connection. It is even possible you might find new friendships here that last forever.'

'I found myself a new friend already,' said Emily as she hugged Prana and they all laughed.

'I had been feeling in pain all morning. I was so focused on my pain and homework that I hardly noticed any of you when you came,' said Jayan. 'But when I opened my eyes, everything had changed. You were like old friends around me. Thank you all for being here with me. I wouldn't have been able to do this without you today.'

'Jayan, visualise the new scene for ten minutes every day, when you wake up and before you go to bed. Keep visualising the waterfall, the pink bubbles, the fun in cleaning the throat with Ganesh and the love in your heart,' said Rose. 'During the day, you can spend some time in silence at the temple and visualise the love spreading inside of you as well as around you. Healing doesn't take place in one day. It is work-in-progress that requires trust, self-love, and patience.'

Jayan nodded gratefully.

****

As she walked under the thick heat of another summer afternoon, Prana found Rose sitting on a bench near the small pond. She was not sure if Rose was meditating or simply admiring the white lotuses. She was about to turn back and leave when Rose looked at her.

'Would you like to join me? I have some time on my hands.'

'I would be very happy for a few minutes with you,' said Prana as she joined her on the bench.

'What's disturbing you? I noticed you walking around a bit restless.'

'After seeing the peaceful transformation in Jayan, I thought I would give it a try. I started a list of significant moments from childhood, but I cannot find anything wrong. My parents have always supported me and showered me with love. They always made the right choices for me, including university. Could you perhaps help me figure out what went wrong?'

Rose took a moment to think before asking, 'If I remember correctly, you are completing a course in law?'

Prana nodded.

'So, tell me, are you passionate about becoming a lawyer?'

'Not really, but as I got on with the course, I felt more confident. After graduation, I will go back to Mauritius and work there.'

'Did you tell your parents that it wasn't your passion?'

'No….,' replied Prana hesitantly. 'I want to live up to their expectations and make them proud.'

'If you were given the chance to choose another profession, what could it be?'

Prana frowned. 'I don't know. I've never thought about it. There has been no need for me to choose.'

'Have there been occasions when you felt resentful towards your parents?'

'Once they prevented me from befriending some girls in high school whom they believed were not good enough. I was angry, but it did not last long as I knew that they were doing their best for me.'

'Let us roll the camera forward to a more recent time when you moved in with James. Was it your choice?'

Prana shook her head. 'No, it was too soon, but he convinced me that it was going to work. I trusted him.'

'You have a kind heart with an inability to say no to others. In an unconscious way, it is more important for you to make other people happy by fulfilling their expectations, and you forget about your own life.'

Prana frowned. 'What's wrong with this if it makes me happy?'

'It didn't last long, did it? You've been living against your heart's desire, like a puppet who is so caught up seeking people's love and approval, that she forgets about her own existence. You don't even know what you want to do in life. It is like having a car but sitting in the backseat while the driver chooses where to take you, and you say yes, even if it is not where you want to go.'

A puppet? Prana felt devastated.

'Unlike Jayan and others who have shared their childhood issues, your problem is that nothing happened for you. You are just a shadow. James is not the result of a pattern in your life, but a wake-up call for you to stand on your own feet. This relationship has brought changes in your life for which you have to assume responsibility now,' said Rose firmly.

Prana felt miserable acknowledging the truth in Rose's words, but she knew that it was in her best interest to carry on this mind-opening conversation.

'Please teach me how to find my own life,' she asked with humility.

Rose nodded. 'Listen carefully. Present-moment awareness is the first step. Accept that what happened is gone. You cannot step into the past and change it. Aryaji recommended that you meditate because you are still prisoner of your past. If you succeed, you will be able to connect with the Universe from a place of authenticity. As you move along this journey, you will also discover your purpose, and everything will fall into place. You cannot step into the future and force it.

'Secondly, love yourself and allow gratitude to flourish in your heart. Self-love is a powerful tool to destroy emotions that poison the body. Guilt is a common one that everyone experiences at some point. Some live and die with it. You are in the right place to nurture yourself and cultivate the patience to wait until your mud settles and your water is clear again. Instead of thinking about what you lost with James, be grateful for what you have. Learn to communicate from the heart, this will enable you to connect with others from a better place. Do you follow me?'

Prana found it hard to grasp all this information in one go, but she wanted more. Her dry heart was soaking it all like a sponge. She nodded.

'Third is forgiveness. Forgiveness can move mountains and sets you free. Individuals are like lighthouses which connect with each other. You are likely to receive what you send. If you are resentful, you can guess what will come back your way. Forgiveness is the key to unconditional love. It is incomplete if you don't let go of guilt and forgive yourself. Self-forgiveness is shedding the last coat that's hiding your shining light. You can then connect to the Universe from a place of compassion and pure selfless love. Fourth is unconditional love. It is too soon to talk about it. You need to go through the first stages to be able to understand the last one.'

'I am not sure I grasped everything. Can you summarize please?'

Rose nodded. 'The first step is to let go of thoughts and stay in the present moment. Secondly, develop self-love and gratitude. Thirdly, forgive others and yourself. It is only then that you will understand love. A combination of these lead to a divine connection from your soul energy to the Universal energy. In simple words, live for what today has to offer not what yesterday has taken away. Happiness is right here.'

Prana's voice trembled. 'James made me believe in a beautiful life together. I was so happy each time he came home. He would look at me with so much love in his eyes. I loved him more than I loved myself.'

'We should always love ourselves first, then we can love others from a healthy place, not from a place of need. The ball is in your court now.'

'I respect your advice. I want true happiness.'

'That's the spirit. Live with passion,' said Rose with a smile.

Prana wondered out loud. 'I have heard a lot about the life force energy since I arrived. Why do we have to go through all these steps when we could feel connected to the Universe simply by awakening our flow of energy?'

'If it was that easy, the world would be a kinder place. You cannot jump from A to Z. First you suffer, next you awaken, then you ascend. These steps are important for an individual to discard unhealthy baggage and be in the right space for being part of the Universal consciousness. You can only enter this place with purity,' said Rose.

Rose placed her hand on Prana's back and rubbed it comfortingly. 'Aruna temple is blessed with ancient knowledge. Being here offers you a golden opportunity to rekindle your life force. You need to trust and go with the flow. If you are scared, know that this fear is coming up for a reason. You hold the key to set it free.'

Prana hugged her as tears poured down her face. 'It is the first time that someone had asked me to do something only for my own benefit.'

'From the first day we met, I could see this desire for life burning in your eyes. It is looking for a way out. Today, you are the one who came to me, in search for answers,' said Rose confidently. 'Whatever you believe to be a burden, is a blessing in disguise. You can do it, Prana.'

****

An hour later, Prana was on her way to the Angel Room. She looked forward to the unexpected one-to-one meditation. She felt so at ease with Rose that she wondered if they had known each other in a past life. But then, Rose was so compassionate that everyone probably felt the same about her. A long candle-light holder was now where the table and chairs had been earlier. Small crystal stones of several colours surrounded the holder. They both sat on cushions facing each other with the candlelight burning in the centre with the light reaching their heart level.

Rose smiled as she wrapped her shawl around her shoulders. 'Are you ready for some fun?'

'I thought we were going to meditate.'

'We will do a visualisation, which is a different type of meditation. We will go in search of treasure.'

'I am ready,' replied Prana.

Rose softened her voice. 'Closing your eyes, take a nice deep breath in .... and sigh it out. As you take a second nice deep breath in, feel your chest expanding like a balloon and breathe out. This process will carry on naturally without you having to do a thing. Now, visualise yourself walking towards a beach with a rucksack on your shoulders. As you go past the palm trees, you feel the warmth of the sunshine on your arms and the gentle breeze on your face. You hear the leaves rustling as they sway graciously. Your feet sink into the soft warm sand as you walk towards the ocean. The sound of the waves helps you relax more and more.

'You notice two boats in the water. As you get closer, you can see *The Past* written on the boat which is to the left. It has been waiting to relieve you from the tiring weight that you have been carrying. You lift the heavy rucksack which contains painful memories that don't serve you any longer. Take it off your shoulders and dump it in the boat!'

Rose paused for a minute. 'What a relief! You feel so much lighter and happier already. Give the boat a push and watch it sail away. And now, turn to the right where there is the other boat named *Bright Future*. You can smell the fresh paint, and it has your name written on it. You step onto the deck, and you can see that the boat is full of fuel and equipped with all the comforts you need. There is also a map to guide you on the best possible path to reach your goals. The energy on board is vibrant and your outstanding boat is ready to sail!

'The sea is calm and inviting. You start the engine and set off on your fantastic journey. As you breathe in the healthy air, your cells and molecules absorb its vitality, right down to the level of consciousness! Your body feels the same stillness as the horizon ahead.'

'You reach your perfect destination and get off the boat. There is an angel waiting for you. He hands you a treasure box with your name written on. Take a deep breath in and open it. You just found the treasure that will help you find happiness. Thank your angel and make your way to the boat. It sails back to this present moment. You are bringing a unique treasure. Remember, you are the navigator of your destiny in every moment.'

'When you are ready, you can gently return your awareness to your body. Wriggle your toes and move your fingers. Stretch your body.'

They stayed in silence, savouring the tranquillity.

'What do people usually find?' asked Prana.

'It can be healing potions, balloons of love, a wedding ring. Someone even came back a millionaire with his boat transformed into a yacht. A person who felt lonely came back with a pet. This is the power of visualisation, it can be anything,' said Rose.

Sadly, Prana said, 'All I found was an oval hand mirror with a silver handle.'

'Wonderful! All gifts are a treasure in some way or another,' exclaimed Rose.

'Although I was holding it in front of me, I could not lift it to look at myself. I tried hard, but it was too heavy. It would not go higher than my heart.'

'The message is clear. You must let go of the heaviness in your heart to find yourself. The mirror will help you see your beauty through your own eyes. You are not yet ready for it, so keep the mirror safely and don't be disheartened. The time will come.'

'I was hoping to find something life changing. Or perhaps new friends who would bring joy into my life.'

'Things, no matter how precious, come and go. People come and go. What you see in the mirror will always reflect what is present.'

Prana could not refute this.

Rose picked up a diary that was next to her and handed it to her.

'What is it?' asked Prana.

'A useful gift. Before you go to bed, make it a habit to write about your day in this diary. When you put your thoughts and emotions on paper, it makes it easier to observe the patterns that prevent you from feeling present. After a while, it will become easier to release energy that stayed caught in the story of the past. At the core of your dreams could be your life purpose.'

'What shall I do when I find it?'

'It will free up space where you can create your future. This will be the day when you will outgrow what you thought you could not live without.'

The world is like a tail of dog, its nature is to curl.
The best you can do is stay quiet
and not let anything bother you…
Visitors will come and go, don't interfere with these waves…
Just be silent…

H.W.L. Poonja (*The Truth Is*)

Chapter 4

The Guru and the Grumpy

As the sun rose over the city of Rishikesh, bringing with it a hint of magic, India was starting to win her heart. The pinkish sky was pierced with golden rays. Prana stood on the small, flowered balcony, soaking in the sunbeams of a wonderful morning. For someone who was not an early riser, she surprised herself by feeling amazingly energetic despite only six hours of sleep. She wanted to make the most of this bonus unexpected time before the yoga class.

The garden stood as still as a postcard. She felt a pang of guilt as the dry leaves rustled under her footsteps upsetting the verdant tranquillity. Cheerful orange marigolds and swaying sunflowers greeted her like old friends as she made her way through the garden to the temple. A group of twelve monks, dressed in white, were already meditating inside. Prana sat discreetly in a corner to start her own meditation. Since she was the only other one there, she felt like an outsider intruding on their privacy and decided to leave. Just as she was about to step outside a roar resonated throughout the temple. She nearly jumped out of her skin. It took her a moment to realise that the monks were laughing. At first their laughter sounded forced, but it swiftly evolved into genuine mirth. Their belly laughs soon turned contagious. Some monks had tears of laughter rolling down their cheeks. Puzzled, she slipped out unnoticed.

'*Everyone is crazy in this country! If I'm not careful I might end up like one of them in this mad house*,' thought Prana, giggling as she made her way to the yoga class. As she had hoped, the Sunshine Room was filled with light. The Eastern wall was a giant window from floor to ceiling. Blue yoga mats lay on the wooden floor. Prana saw only new faces as she settled on a mat.

'Namaste, everyone. I'm Nathan. I've been teaching yoga at the temple for 3 years now,' said the young teacher sitting at the front of the room. He looked immaculate with neatly trimmed chestnut hair, tanned skin, and incredibly clear blue eyes. He matched an orange t-shirt with loose blue jogging bottoms that looked brand new, still showing the creases of an outfit which had just been unpacked. 'If you are ready, we will soon begin.'

'We'll start with some gentle warming up postures to awaken the senses. Your body has been in pause mode during your sleep. It is time to increase the blood flow and bring it back to life,' he said. He stood up and began swinging his arms from side to side.

A few sounds were uttered as the group joined in, with unconscious groans and sighs. As they stretched their upper bodies, they soon felt looser and carried on with forward bends. Prana felt her body getting warmer as they moved on to standing, then gentle bending postures. Nathan walked around, helping those who struggled. Prana was confused when he held her right arm to straighten it. '*It was already straight*,' she thought.

Prana listened attentively and tried to imitate Nathan's examples. She was particularly challenged by the *surya namaskars* postures. It was difficult to control breathing and movements at the same time. The middle-aged lady in front of her gave up and sat on her mat watching the others.

Nathan encouraged them in his cheerful voice. 'If you do these postures six times every morning, you will release a burst of energy for the whole day. These stretches will make your body feel more balanced. Concentrate on the moment with each movement that you make. You might even feel younger after a while.'

He was very likeable with his easy-going and positive attitude.

'Is this your secret to looking young and handsome?' asked a white-haired lady.

Nathan flashed a broad smile. 'I don't know about that, but I can definitely say that yoga keeps the body in shape and calms the mind. It can bring hours of peace.'

After fifty minutes of hard work, which Nathan called 'gentle' hatha yoga, they lay down on their mats for relaxation.

'We will complete the class with a short meditation, the *present moment awareness*. It is a simple practice that brings the mind to rest. It helps us to be in a centred and comfortable space,' he said.

'Close your eyes and take a slow deep breath in and sigh it out. Inhale slowly as you count to eight, hold your breath for a count of four, then exhale as you count to eight again.'

Nathan's voice was so smooth, it could make a restless child fall asleep. 'Feel your abdomen expand as you breathe in. Focus on the heartbeat when you hold your breath. As you breathe out, feel your belly going down like a deflated balloon.'

The breathing exercise lasted five minutes. Towards the end, a few snores could be heard across the room. Nathan allowed them to lie in silence for a few more minutes.

'You may now bring your attention back to the whole body. Wriggle your fingers and toes, stretch the body, and open your eyes when you are ready,' said Nathan. When everyone was sitting again, he asked, 'How was it?'

'I could only count up to five, but I feel more relaxed. Since the class started, I have not thought once of my problems,' said a woman.

Nathan smiled. 'This is what yoga teaches us. When we stay focused in our actions, even the mind becomes engaged with the activity and it has no time to worry.'

'It was up to seven counts for me but then I fell asleep after the fourth breath. This morning, I woke up feeling irritable after a disturbed sleep, but now I am refreshed,' said a man, giving a thumbs up.

'Very good! Practice makes perfect. If you do it every day, your breathing will become better paced and you will be able to reach up to ten counts or perhaps even more,' replied Nathan with a nod.

'Yoga must be boring after a while. Surely all the classes are pretty much the same?' asked a man grumpily.

'There is no chance of this ever happening. Do you ever get bored of breathing? Yoga is about breath, the flow of energy and movement in the body. There are over a thousand poses which leave no space for boredom. We are constantly learning,' replied Nathan.

He turned to Prana. 'I noticed that you were frowning a few times. Was there something on your mind?'

Prana hated to admit it. 'Sadly, yes.'

'There are times when our mind is so used to being in charge that neither meditation nor deep breathing works,' explained Nathan. 'The best solution is to ask for assistance from Mother Nature. Go for a walk, and with every step, let all your thoughts come up. Keep walking and thinking. Ask all the thoughts to come as if you are inviting them to a party. When you stop pushing them away, they get bored of coming and eventually stop.'

Prana eyed him suspiciously.

Nathan smiled. 'Trust me, your focus will move back to your movements, making you feel grounded. You will become more aware of your footsteps and your heartbeat as it gets faster.'

'What if it doesn't work?' said Prana.

'What if it works?' replied the yoga *guru* persuasively. 'If you don't trust your potential, you make your journey hard. Kirtana's *The Train Song* describes it beautifully: *Trains of thoughts will come and go, but you are not these thoughts you know, so why get all caught up in where they lead? You are who these thoughts are passing through – don't you see?*'

'I will give it a try', replied Prana.

'You will see, the best feeling in the world is watching things fall back into place after watching them fall apart for so long.'

The white-haired lady, who by now was not hiding her crush on Nathan, said, 'I don't mind giving you my phone number if you are always so cool.'
'Sorry to disappoint you, aunty,' replied Nathan with a wink. 'I have my own worries, just like everyone else. We are all working on our own issues, except for the few enlightened masters. It's time to wrap up lovely people! I hope to see you all tomorrow for another session.'

****

Prana had no problem finding Emily for breakfast. Her new friend stood out in her sleeveless lime-coloured dress. Even her bright lipstick was easy to spot from a distance. Emily was already halfway through a *thali* of masala dosa accompanied with its small bowls of lentils and chutney. There was a plate with two aloo parathas next to it and a glass of lassi. Her clothes looked a size too small, but she did not seem to mind as she happily cleared her plates.
'How was the yoga?' she asked as Prana joined her.
'Amazing! I think it has set me for a stunning day ahead.'
'This sounds promising. I might come tomorrow. Is this all you will eat?'
Despite the wide variety of typical Indian breakfast, Prana had settled for a bowl of porridge, fruit salad and a cup of coffee. 'Spicy food doesn't sit very well with my stomach. Besides, I don't eat much in the morning.' She thought it was better to skip the part of the food that was making her sick these days.
They had almost finished breakfast when Prana recognised a tall and slim man approaching their table. He was the one who found yoga boring and grumbled to himself with each new posture earlier on. He looked austere with his angular face and strong jawlines. His greying hair suggested he could be in his fifties. Prana wondered if he had got out of bed on the wrong side that morning.
'Do you mind if I join you?' he asked and sat without waiting for an answer. 'I am John from London. I am just so busy with clients that my brother suggested I come here to relax. This place is a total waste of time. Take the yoga class, for instance. There's nothing that I could not have done in my *large* apartment.' He paused to ascertain that they caught the word large, 'having said this, I hate to admit that my brother could be right for a change. My business is so successful that I hardly have time to spare for myself, let alone anyone else.'
Prana and Emily looked at each other, lost for words. It was clear that John had joined them only to boast about himself.
'You both look too young to be successful. I can give you some tips for a bright future,' he carried on arrogantly.
Emily interrupted him. 'If we concentrate on work too early, we might miss out on some joys in life. These cannot be brought back with time, no matter how much money one may have.'

'You need to learn how to take charge early, to control not only your life but also the lives of the people in your circle of influence,' replied John in a disapproving tone.

'My father owns a successful agency in Malaysia. It does not prevent him from being kind and respectful of others,' said Emily, hoping that would be enough to make John leave.

'This explains why you are so overweight,' said John with a hint of contempt. 'If your father had been firmer, today you would probably know how much to eat and how to dress better.'

Emily stared with an open mouth and put down the piece of paratha she had been eating.

'Oh sorry, did I offend you? I am an honest man,' muttered John as he stood up. 'If you'll excuse me, I have another busy day ahead.'

He gave them a smug smile before joining another table of people.

Emily's eyes filled with tears. She pushed away her plate and wiped the bit of butter that was on her lips with a napkin.

Prana tried to comfort her. 'That was outrageous. Honey, it's easy to tell that he is a lonely and arrogant man. Ignore him.'

'At times from the way people look at me, I know that they are thinking that I am fat, and it is true, but no one has ever been nasty to me,' said Emily.

Prana held her hand. 'Forget about him. He will soon be kicked out of here with such a rude attitude. Don't let him spoil your stay.'

Prana could feel someone's eyes fixed on her as they completed their breakfast in silence. She glanced towards the food area and noticed the old lady behind the tea counter staring at her with intense black eyes. She was dressed in a plain grey saree. Prana smiled at her, but she did not smile back. Instead, she carried on pouring tea in mugs.

'*Strange people everywhere*,' thought Prana.

****

Magnificent fields that belonged to the temple extended over 200 acres. Prana had read in the leaflet that Aruna temple operated with a philosophy of conscious living promoted by devotion to Mother Nature through organic cultivation. The fields were split into three colourful sections of fruits, vegetables, and herbs. The fresh aromas blended with each other and spread a mixed sense of lightness to the place. When the wind blew, it occasionally brought with it a whiff of cow dung from the adjoining sheds. She had been impatiently waiting for this opportunity to join in one of the local activities.

Native men and women were busy hand-picking tulsi leaves. The women had their heads covered with their sarees to protect themselves from the sun. Their silver nose rings and anklets shone in the sunlight. Some smiled at the foreigners who joined them while others kept their heads down and peeped shyly. The men were more outgoing with some of them singing out loud in their native *Hindi*. They had dark chocolate coloured skin that had wrinkled over years of working under the fiery sun. They happily showed off their skill by walking around with heavy baskets swaying comfortably on their heads. They worked together as a friendly community.

Noisy tourists and quieter companions from the temple mingled, eager to share the experience. The bolder ones carried their basket on their heads while the cautious ones had it strapped over their backs. They were all wearing hats or had a long piece of cloth wrapped around their head to protect them from sunburn. A white heavily built man looked weird with a fading blue head-cloth, the basket overstretched on his back to the point of bursting and a pair of Oakley sunglasses. A tiny woman was struggling to keep up in her high heels. However, everyone seemed to be having fun like school kids on an adventure. There were giggles when tourists tried to join in the folklore singing. The natives were happily demonstrating how to find the best tulsi leaves.

Prana was relieved that Emily seemed to have forgotten about John. She was back to her happy nature, humming as they filled their baskets with shiny purple eggplants.

'I wonder what they are doing over there,' said Emily as she pointed towards some people strolling a bit further from the field.

Prana knew straightaway. 'They are connecting with Mother Nature to feel more present in the moment.'

'Did you just make that up?'

'No, I learnt it this morning. If you come to yoga, you'll soon become wiser.'

Emily burst out laughing. 'I think you should stop going to this class or else you'll turn into a boring old monk.'

'You will like the teacher. He's funny,' said Prana.

They soon headed towards the farm with their baskets filled to the brim with eggplants. Other people were already there with potatoes, bitter gourds, lady fingers, cucumbers, ginger and tulsi leaves. Everyone got quieter as the heat took its toll on them. Helpers were serving refreshments with one hand while skilfully pushing flies away from the glasses with the other. People sat around appreciating their drinks.

While they queued up waiting for their turn, Emily elbowed Prana in the arm. 'Check out the guy sitting straight ahead. He looks like he stepped straight out from the pages of a fashion magazine!'

Prana glanced at him and suppressed a smile. 'I totally agree!'

'He's waving at us,' said Emily, waving back.

'Let's join him and you can ask him why he came to Aruna,' said Prana as she chose a fresh melon juice to soothe the dryness in her throat.

Nathan was leaning back in a plastic chair, looking very relaxed. 'I can see that you ladies have been working hard,' he said as they approached.

Emily sat down. 'Unlike you, mister. Are you a tourist relaxing here?'

'No, my afternoon work starts after yours is done. I deliver the vegetables, fruits, and milk to the temple. And later when the meals are ready, I take some to the local orphanage down in the village.'

'What a contrast to your morning work,' said Prana.

'What work? Did I miss something?' asked Emily. She pulled a banana oat bar from her small bag and started munching passionately.

Prana laughed. 'Nathan is the yoga teacher.'

'Really?' asked Emily, baffled.

Nathan nodded. 'Yes, but why are you so surprised?'

'I think you look too young to be doing an old man's job,' confessed Emily.

'Yoga is a discipline, not a job.'

'See what this job has done to you – you sound like an old man!'

'What do you mean? I only just turned 35. I am an old soul in a young body.' He pretended to sound hurt as he ran his hand through his hair.

'I have been trying hard to convince Emily to come tomorrow morning, but no luck so far. She might listen to you,' said Prana.

'I will join a class,' came the reply before Nathan even opened his mouth.

'Are you going for the class or for the teacher?' teased Prana.

Emily giggled. 'Hey, don't get any false ideas. You know I have a boyfriend. Besides, I can tell that Nathan already has his eyes fixed on someone,' she said, looking at Nathan mischievously.

Nathan ignored her comment. 'He is lucky to have a sweet girlfriend like you.'

'You should tell him that. I can't remember the last time he complimented me. We made a deal recently about me losing weight,' replied Emily. 'If you'll both excuse me, I need another juice.' She left, lost in her thoughts.

Prana was happy that someone had been nice to Emily. She was intrigued by Nathan. There was something distinct about him.

'Come with me. I will show you the best area for meditating in nature,' offered Nathan.

Although she was already exhausted, Prana put down her empty glass and they made their way to the other side of the farm.

'Is this trip a part of your holidays in India?' asked Nathan.

Prana matched his pace as they walked side by side. 'I guess you could call it a spiritual holiday. My life took an unexpected turn when I was studying in London. I knew that it was time for me to leave. I came here for guidance.'

'You're certainly in the right place,' said Nathan with approval. 'Did you come alone?'

Prana nodded. She thought that she noticed a flicker of joy in Nathan's eyes as she looked at him but brushed it aside. '*The heat must be giving me illusions*,' she thought.

'I have been trying in vain to pin down your accent. Where are you from?' she asked.

'Australia,' replied Nathan. 'I have been living in India for five years now. I fell in love with the people, the teachings, and the country. It has totally changed my perception of life, and it hasn't stopped astonishing me.'

'Were you already teaching yoga before you came?'

'Oh, far from it…' said Nathan with a sigh. 'I used to be a rebellious teenager. Back then I was on strong drugs, so I could fit in the cool groups of guys at school. Before I knew it, I was a heavy drug addict. I failed my finals and fell into depression when my friends moved on to college. Although my parents tried to help and loved me dearly, I was stuck in a gloomy world. I could see their despair, but it was impossible for me to connect with them. I was depressed and for me, emotions did not exist.'

He got distracted by the squawk of birds flying past. He went quiet as he followed them with his eyes until they were out of sight.

'You don't need to tell me more if it's upsetting you,' said Prana kindly, even though she hoped he would continue.

Nathan had a sip of water from a bottle that he took with him. 'My parents sent me to a rehabilitation centre. It was like a living hell. I would scream, cry, and beg for drugs but all I got was tasteless food, water, and fresh juice. Everything was tasteless. After months of counselling, I saw that if I kept on fighting this change, I would be fighting my whole life. It was time to say goodbye to the illusion of my old comforting life and embrace the challenging future. I started reading *The Power of Now* and that had a powerful effect on me. My body and mind gradually cleared up. My ghost-like complexion was replaced by a healthier appearance.'

Nathan looked at Prana and smiled. 'Soon, I felt alive again. I joined the local community service and I felt useful as I helped children in an orphanage. It was a rewarding sensation when they thanked me for telling them stories, for playing football or when they held my hand to show me around. It was the first time in years that I felt emotions which I forgot existed. My parents were delighted that they found me again.'

'It must have been a true gift to feel this connection again.'

'Absolutely. I accompanied my mum to her yoga and meditation classes. I was looking for a healthy replacement, something that would keep me busy during my free moments when I might feel temped to start doing drugs again. I was in complete awe when I discovered this infinite space within me. I was thirsty for more. I went every week, but my thirst for more remained unquenched. I woke up every morning with the same question – *who am I*?'

They reached a narrow pathway. Prana followed Nathan and they were soon walking between trees. Nathan stopped in an area that was protected from the sun by the leafy branches. Prana felt her body starting to cool down as she sat on the fresh earth and pushed her sandals away.

Nathan rolled up his sleeves and sat resting his back against a trunk. 'I can stop if it's too much information.'

'Please carry on. Why did you leave if you were happy?' asked Prana, captivated by his story.

'I received a message when I was meditating one morning. It was only one word, and it was clear. *INDIA*. I knew straightaway that this was the place for me. It was hard for my parents when I left, but they understood and respected my decision.'

'When I saw you in the class, I thought that you were so joyful because you have always had an easy life. I admire your journey even more now that I know how hard it's been for you.'

'The journey to finding oneself can often be a tough one. My mum still says that she got her son back from drugs but then lost him to India. I miss my family, but this is my path now.'

Prana discerned a touch of nostalgia in his voice. 'How often do you visit them?'

'I only went back once. I don't want to fall back into those dark years. My heart is here, where I experience stillness.'

'Are you scared that you might fall back into depression?' asked Prana, surprised.

'I keep building up my inner strength to progress on my spiritual path, but I have my own ghosts from the past. I feel exposed when I am there. I am human,' said Nathan gently.

He looked so vulnerable that Prana wanted to reach out and hug him, but she held back. She admired him even more for his honesty.

'What a contrast. Your parents lost you, but it is the opposite for me,' she said, thinking out loud.

'What do you mean?' asked Nathan.

'When I was studying in England, I moved in with my British boyfriend. Things went wrong after a while, and we broke up. I hesitate to go back home. I come from a religious family where my behaviour will be considered shameful. My parents still think that I am still studying in London,' replied Prana.

'This is part of your past now, let it go. You don't even need to tell your parents about it,' reassured Nathan.

Prana could not stop the tears. The familiar sinking feeling in the pit of her stomach was back. She trusted Nathan and wanted to tell him more, but she was too scared to see this understanding in his eyes turn to disapproval.

Nathan gave her his handkerchief. 'It is never too late to set things right. If you feel like you are losing everything, remember that trees lose their leaves every winter, but they still stand tall and wait for spring to come.'

'It's not that easy.'

He pulled her close and Prana rested her head on his shoulder.

'You don't have to say anything more,' he said softly.

Prana felt safe as she closed her eyes and relaxed in his embrace. Although this was new, she felt like she had found a long-lost friend in Nathan. They sat for a while, enjoying the comfortable silence of the surroundings and the sound of the chirping birds.

Nathan pulled back, reluctantly. 'Now is the perfect moment for you to practise focusing on the breathing. Have some time on your own in this refreshing space. You can then go for a walk on the other side of the field. Try not to fight your thoughts but welcome them like old friends.'

She gave him a grateful smile.

He squeezed her hand before getting up and making his way back.

****

Dear Diary,

I am grateful to God for bringing wonderful people like Rose, Emily, and Nathan in my life.

I must tell them the truth before they find out for themselves. I won't be able to hide this for long.

God please give me the strength to speak the truth.

You must go and sit inside the cave of your own heart.
When you can bear your own emptiness – you are free.

Mooji

Chapter 5

Is your Sanctum Sacred or Scared? Satsang

Aryaji was already in the room when Prana arrived for satsang. He could have been mistaken for a statue, sitting cross-legged, staring straight ahead. He was wearing a peach-coloured silk kurta and was holding a string of amethyst crystal prayer beads on his lap. She wondered how long it had taken him to reach this stage of spirituality. His eyes looked wider with his hair tied at the back.

It had been three days since she last attended a satsang. She did not attend all of them as it was not restricted to the retreat, and also welcomed people from the local area, so she did not understand everything that was shared in the local language. Prana was tempted to walk to Aryaji and touch his face to test if he could preserve his open-eye trance meditation. Instead, she sat next to Emily. She spotted John in the last row with his arms crossed across over his chest, looking impatient even before the session had started. He looked out of place with his black shirt and tie. '*How come he is still here?*' she thought.

Aryaji's voice floated, welcoming and friendly. 'Namaste, dear friends. When people are asked what they want in life, the answer is often, *to be happy*. Today let us explore the magic of happiness. I am sure that all of you want to be happy!'

There was loud agreement and nods.

'The main ingredient to create happiness is love and its biggest enemy is fear. Experiences of love during childhood influence our ability to love ourselves and others as we grow up. The more there is love, the more happiness gets generated in our private sanctum,' explained Aryaji.

'Where is this sanctum?' asked Prana.

'It is an inner place where you feel safe. You create it using your imagination. It is a peaceful and beautiful place. It can be in nature where you have a lake, a forest, a beach, a garden, or a mountain. It can be in spring or summer when the birds are singing, the scent of colourful flowers teases your nostrils, and the sky is blue. You feel the warmth of the sun on your arms and a gentle breeze your face. It can be anywhere your imagination wants to take you, that's the beauty of your own creation.'

He closed his eyes for a moment, searching for something in his own mind of knowledge.

'Today we will go through an exercise as a guide to creating your own private sanctum. When you are ready, close your eyes, take a few deep breaths in through the nose, and let them out through the mouth. Relax your shoulders and let your body sink in the chair.

'Now, imagine you are in a garden. There is the most fabulous house you have ever seen in the middle of this garden. What is it made of? Is it timber wood? Or maybe marble stone? What is the shape? Feel the soft green grass beneath your feet as you walk towards it. You can smell the flowers and you are fascinated by the richly coloured tulips. Only you can step into this house as the door will only open when you stand in front of it. Are you there now? Great…. You feel a new connection in your heart already as you walk in and close the door behind you. It's like being at home.

'Inside, it is still empty, waiting for you to decorate. Make it a unique place where you feel safe and happy. Choose your favourite colours, furniture, and some cushions. Is there a radio that plays soothing songs and meditations? Or maybe a warm fireplace with a thick blanket spread in front, waiting to embrace you in its warmth? You can hang pictures with peaceful sceneries on the walls. Make yourself comfortable. This is your new home.

'This special place makes you happy both inside and outside. This is your sanctum, your eternal home filled with love. Bask in this loving energy. You are at peace here. Enjoy your journey in this space for a few minutes in silence until I call you back.

The room was in silence as Aryaji allowed them to carry on with the visualisation.

'You are now ready to leave, knowing that you can visit anytime and make it even more special each time you come. No one can disturb your energy there … Slowly bring your awareness back to the room. Have a gentle stretch and open your eyes when you are ready.'

There were a few sighs as people stretched.

'There are forty of us here today and I am sure that we had forty different sanctums. Who would like to share their experience?' asked Aryaji, with a smile.

'Mine was amazing. As I was walking to a wooden cottage, I realised it was the same one I used to live in when I was a child. I had totally forgotten about it or what it looked like inside, so I decorated it the way I would want it now,' said a man who was sitting on a cushion with his back resting against the wall. His eyes shone like a child who had found his favourite lost toy.

'This is the power of positive thinking combined with imagination. Well done,' said Aryaji before adding, 'No matter how old we are, we all have an inner child. From the moment we are born, he has been waiting for his special home where he will be loved and happy. Many of you present here today have been deprived of this love in your early years. It may happen that as you grew up, you didn't give it much importance anymore. An ignore button is pressed to discard the sadness, consciously or subconsciously. As time goes, a sense of emptiness grows where happiness should have been. Fear starts to fill this empty space. Fear of loving in case it is not reciprocated. Fear of being happy in case it is taken away.

'If we are not alert, fear spreads in our whole being, at a cellular level and can turn into panic. It sounds dangerous, but most fears are non-existent. They are simply thoughts that we can get rid of.'

A woman from the second row raised her hand. Her voice was shaky, 'How does one get rid of fear?'

'Take a fight, for example. There are two opponents waiting to fight each other. One is thinking about turning and running away as he fears for his life. The other one is just as scared, but he decides to fight for his life.'

'It is safer to run away,' she said.

'That's what you might think. If you run away from fear, it will hunt you down and show up again in some way or another. The only way to be free from fear is by facing it until it dissolves.'

'Maybe this explains why I don't know where to go when I feel scared,' she said.

'Would you like to tell us more?' asked Aryaji as he signalled to Nathan to pass her the mic.

She stood up, tall and scared. Her hands were shaking as she took the mic. Her face was surrounded with whitish blonde curls. 'My name is Heidi. I am fifty years old, and I come from Germany. I am here for the retreat. I used to lead a normal life. I was one of the most productive and confident employees in the agency where I worked. My sales figures were always at the top.'

She took a deep breath and wiped the beads of sweat that had formed on her forehead. 'Three months ago, I lost my job. My confidence was shattered, and I was scared about not finding another job. At first, I felt better by listening to some music that helped me doze off. I applied for new jobs and although I was called for interviews, none were successful. I think that they could tell I was not confident. I started having panic attacks and needing to leave the lights on when I went to bed. Soon after, I stopped receiving interview offers and the panic attacks got worse. I might never get a job now.'

Aryaji responded with a soft smile. 'Your fear had turned into an abnormal fear from constant worrying. Your imagination is running in all directions like a wild cat.'

'I want to be the successful person I used to be. I have heard a lot about how people who want to find their way again in life have been able to do so by coming here. I am ready to do what it takes.'

Aryaji looked at her for a while. 'Do nothing then. Has it ever occurred to you that maybe your path is meant to be different? What if you are not supposed to be doing sales in the first place?'

'I think that you did not understand my problem. I am a professional,' came the frustrated reply.

'What if this was not the truth?'

'What do you mean?'

'Maybe you are meant to be doing something else.'

'I know what I should be doing. All I need to know is how to stop the panic attacks. I want to be the strong and confident person I used to be,' replied Heidi aggressively.

'What if they never stop?' said Aryaji, with a hint of mystery in his voice.

'Then I wasted my time coming here!' shouted Heidi.

Her rage cut through the room like a razor. Some people looked at each other with concern.

Aryaji seemed amused by her tone. 'Heidi, your confidence is back! Your hands are holding the mic firmly now. Your voice is loud and clear. I can see sparkles of determination in your eyes. Where has the shaking fear gone?'

His trick had worked. He had astutely shifted Heidi's attention from her story to the present moment. The room was silent, waiting for Heidi's reaction. She stood still, with her eyes alert and her body tense, waiting for the shaking to start again.

Aryaji was not in a rush to fill in the silence.

He waited with her. Everyone waited.

Nothing happened.

Heidi's body gradually started to relax.

'See, you can do it!' His tone was reassuring, calm and serious.

She looked at him and started to giggle. She put her hands in front of her mouth and tried to stop but burst out laughing. She held on to her stomach that was hurting from laughter. If anyone had walked in at that precise moment, they would have thought that she was either drunk or mad. Her laughter was contagious and the whole room was soon laughing.

Heidi wiped the tears that rolled down her cheeks, blushing with shame as she looked at Aryaji. 'I apologise for my childish reaction. I feel so stupid now.'

'Everything is welcome here. Besides, I like children,' he said affectionately. 'They are willing to learn. All you must do now is keep your mind still and see what comes up from your deeper self. Fear is a beautiful test.'

'I don't even know why I feel this uncontrolled laughter!'

'Your body has released some strong stuck emotions. The relief is expressing itself.'

'Thank you for showing me how it is possible to let go of fear. However, it happened easily with your help and the positive energy around. How do I pass the test when I will be on my own?'

'Each time you feel scared, think of fear as a paper tiger in front of you and start tearing the paper, then burn it. Rose will guide you in a session.' He paused before adding, 'Now tell me, when you lost your job, did you talk about it to your friends and family?'

'No, I don't have anyone close, but this did not bother me as my life used to be very busy. Occasionally, I felt a bit alone, but I would do some work and life went on same as before.'

'Life gets mechanical if we don't know how to take a break from the cycle and have happy moments, both on our own and with others. Are you scared to be happy?'

Heidi sighed. 'I don't know. Do I even know what happiness is? My life used to be a rollercoaster with nothing to be happy or sad about. Don't get me wrong, I was happy when I went beyond my sales target, but it was more out of pride. I would mark the moment with a glass of wine in the evening.'

'Could it be because you are scared of happiness that there is nothing around to make you happy? Before going to bed tonight, think about moments in your childhood when you might have felt rejected. Times when you wanted to share something that made you happy, but no one was there to listen,' recommended Aryaji.

'I will,' said Heidi firmly. 'Earlier, I found it difficult to create a happy inner sanctum. All I could think of was my old office. I had to keep the lights on inside and I managed to play some soothing music to help me relax. Did you mean it when you said that it might not be my path to work in an office?'

The master nodded. 'It might be time for new opportunities, but you have to find out for yourself if this is true. You are in automatic thinking mode. Erase it. Feel instead of think. Be still and the answer will naturally come up at the right time. It might not be what you expect … So, hold no expectation whatsoever!'

'Thank you,' replied Heidi, before sitting down.

Aryaji turned his attention back to everyone. 'Here is an exercise to practise when you are alone. Sit in a comfortable place and think of situations from your childhood up to now when you felt unloved. If anything comes up, join Rose for assistance in dissolving emotions that are of no value anymore.'

'Why does it have to be from childhood?' asked one of them.

'Good question. Unhappy patterns develop over the years. They bring their friend, fear. These get anchored in the subconscious mind and create a barrier between our conscious mind and our private sanctum.'

'I could come up with a long list,' said a lady.

'Excellent! They need to go!' exclaimed Aryaji. 'You can do it with courage and a positive attitude. It is time to claim back your right to be happy. Create your private sanctum!'

Time flew by as people shared their experiences. The energy was compassionate in the room until a voice resonated, loud and sarcastic.

'I have been wasting my time listening to all this nonsense,' said John, standing up abruptly. 'It is pathetic how all of you complain like kids!'

A wave of shock swept through the room.

Aryaji spoke quietly. 'Interesting, very interesting … Tell us more about you.'

'As most of you already know, I am John the founder of a worldwide prominent software company. I am rich and successful. My brother thought that I needed a break from my years of hard work. He should have thought twice before arranging my trip to waste my time here,' he responded with a sneer.

'Believe me, it is your own soul that brought you here,' said Aryaji with genuine warmth.

'Pfff … What soul? What sanctum? Can you show them to me? They do not exist!'

'You breathe in air. Can you see it? No, yet it is omnipresent.'

John was getting more irritated. 'The point I want to make is that there is no need for relationships or what you call sanctums, to be happy. My bank accounts are my sanctums. I live alone, and yet I am not lonely. I've had six partners over the past two years, and I am happier after they leave. Good riddance! They were only after my money.'

Aryaji rubbed his chin with his thumb, casually. 'One day, if the bank burns down and all your money disappears, there will be no one around for you.'

His serenity inflamed John's temper even more. 'Nonsense!'

Aryaji kept on poking his ego. 'You sound a little bit upset, John. Is it because you are not in control of our conversation? You should be able to pull yourself together if you think that you are superior to everyone else here.'

John's face went red, on the verge of exploding. 'What do you know about power? You don't own anything of value.'

Aryaji stood up slowly, tall, and strong. 'There is power and there is inner strength. If power comes from the ego, it does not last long. True power starts with inner strength, from a clear heart and a positive mind. Don't undermine the power of what takes place in Aruna. At times people who think they are invincible break down here; while others who thought they were weak discover they can move mountains.'

'I am an invincible mountain, in full control of my life.'

'Is it fear of failure that creates your need to control?'

'I am fearless,' said John, sharply.

'In that case, I have a challenge for you,' said Aryaji. 'Stay three more days. During this time, your phone and your laptop will be taken away and kept safely. You will not talk to anyone.'

John was taken aback but pulled himself back together quickly. 'This is easy. No one here is up to an educated conversation, anyway.'

With a smile, Aryaji said, 'If you think so, accept my challenge. You will be in full control of your life for 36 hours with no one to disturb you.'

'What will I get from it?'

'Your ego will be proud to know that it has been right all the time. You will confirm that money is enough to keep a person happy.'

John's peacock pride felt stabbed. A roomful was waiting for his reply.

'I accept your challenge. Be ready to apologise!', he said.

He walked out without waiting for a reply, banging the door behind him.

The room got noisy with unhappy comments.

Aryaji clapped his hands together to get their attention back. 'Relax, everyone. John left so quickly that I did not have time to thank him for his sharing. He taught us an important lesson today ... how one's ego can affect their behaviour. The stronger the ego, the more limited is the vision.'

'He was very rude! It is unacceptable,' said Mandeep, an elderly man.

'His ego felt threatened and was rebelling. John can only see what the limited ego wants him to see, so he was oblivious of everyone around him. He lives in his own self-important world. He has his own pain. But let's not forget that, just like all of us, he has his own lessons to learn. It is not visible yet, but his negative attitude started shifting the moment he set foot in Aruna.'

Mandeep frowned. 'Even if it is his brother who made him come?'

'His brother was just an instrument in the process. It is a higher force who decided that the time has come for his spiritual journey to begin.'

'What if he is able to prove that money is enough to be happy?' asked Emily, anxiously.

Aryaji smiled. 'Then I will apologise. But, for a man like John who is always busy, three days of silence will be more like three months of torture. He needs to have people around as it is by putting them down that he can confirm his superiority. When left on his own, his ego will feel threatened.'

'I would love to see him tortured.'

'Emily, John needs our compassion. Heated conversations often take place during satsangs. It is normal for strong emotions to arise, especially fear, anger, and sadness,' explained Aryaji. 'With nothing to do, John's mind will slow down, and questions will arise. His ego will feel threatened. An inner battle will start between his ego and his soul. He can choose to run away or face his fear of truth.'

'What if he doesn't come back?'

'It will mean that he is not ready.'

'Please tell us more about the ego,' asked Mandeep. His face was so wrinkled that his stretched eyes were like two dried raisins when opened.

'We all have our own ego which prevents us from experiencing *moksha,* eternal freedom. We are free from ego when it collapses like a deflated balloon, liberating us from life and death. Our kundalini consciousness is released from the base of our spine and connects us to the blissful Universal consciousness.'

'My search for freedom started twenty years ago,' said Mandeep. 'I followed what well-known yogis did to achieve moksha. I lived in ashrams, meditated for hours on mountains, and spent days fasting. I often feel my life force rising from the base of my spine through my chakras, hot and vibrant, but it slows down and stops in my forehead chakra. Why am I not attaining liberation?'

'Who is seeking liberation? Your soul or your ego?' asked Aryaji.

'I have no ego left.'

'Ah! The *I* is the ego talking. It is amazing how *ego* leads us to believe that we got rid of it, while it is still lurking in the dark with the remote control to our soul.'

'I don't know what else to do. I am too old to start all over again,' said Mandeep in despair.

'You don't have to start again. In fact, you have nothing to do. Today could be the day everything changes Mandeep. It could happen any day. The problem is that you are holding on to the expectation of it happening so badly that it is manifesting more expectation.'

'Do you mean it is my ego expecting it to happen?'

'You got it! Next time you sit for meditation, whether it is in an ashram, on a mountain or in your bedroom, sit with faith not expectation. Observe the energy that is present. Let it go where it wants to go in its own time. If your ego tries too hard to get it to the crown chakra, it won't happen.'

Mandeep did a namaste sign as a thank you and simply closed his eyes and sat in silence.

Prana stood up. 'Aryaji, on several occasions, I have been able to experience staying in the present moment. It works better when I am in nature. I noticed that when I write my thoughts in a diary before meditating, it becomes easier to let go.'

'Wonderful Prana! I can already see the change in your aura. When you came, it was a dull pink, trapped in the cobweb of your past. Thin rays of light pink are peeping through now. Keep practising awareness and you will feel the warm energy awakening at the base of your spine.'

'However, I freeze to the core when a pitch-black hole appears. It keeps getting closer and bigger, like a scary black leopard waiting to pounce on me.'

'Let it come. It carries all the pain, guilt, and resentment that you are holding on to.'

'Do I have to go through it all again before finding happiness?'

Aryaji nodded reassuringly. 'Your true sanctum is on the other side. I get a sense that your key to the other side of this black hole is self-love. Happiness comes from the stillness of a heart that is free from harmful feelings, most importantly, from self-harm. It seems that a part of you believes it deserves this misery, perhaps as a form of punishment?' said Aryaji, raising an eyebrow.

Prana felt the hairs on her arms rise.

'Are you guilty about being happy?'

This remark hit too close to home, making her heart pound.

'I haven't thought about this,' she lied.

'Meditate on it then. It might bring up something,' said Aryaji, before turning his attention to the group.

'Some of you might have worked on yourselves already, be free from old pain but are still unhappy. Why is that? Any idea?'

He looked around.

'Could it be because I still don't totally believe that I deserve to be happy?' replied someone.

'Good answer. It doesn't matter if it is a piece of cake that you want or if you are seeking enlightenment, if you don't believe that it can be yours, it will never be yours. You can pick up unhealthy beliefs at any point in life. I know a little boy whose mum used to tell him that he was useless. It happened when he spilt a cup of milk on the floor, got some bad grades or got his new shoes muddy … things that kids usually do. By the time he was six, he totally believed that he was useless. This thought had formed a neural connection with his genes and sunk deeper in his DNA. He grew up feeling the same at work and in relationships.'

Aryaji cleared his throat and had some water before carrying on.

'As layers of unhealthy beliefs pile up, they take us further from self-love, self-confidence, and happiness. We end up living the way other people have labelled us because we believe them more than we believe in our true potential.'

He looked at Heidi. 'Remember this dear one, if you can't find happiness even when you create your inner sanctum. Ask yourself, what belief is holding me back?'

'Today's satsang has been very powerful. We will end our session with a short meditation.'

The mind is a bundle of thoughts, just as a book is a collection of pages.

If each page of the book is torn out, there will no longer be a book.

In the same way, if each thought wave is calmed, the mind will cease to exist.

The temple of your heart takes over.

Imagine that your heart is a lake.

When the surface of a lake is still you can see to the bottom clearly. When it is agitated, this is impossible.

The same is true of the heart. When it is still you can feel peace and love.

Someone has dropped a large, beautiful diamond into the lake of your heart.

To see the diamond at the bottom of the lake, make the breath very slow and smooth so that there are no ripples left on the surface.

As the heart becomes calmer, thoughts will disperse.

Focus all your attention on seeing the diamond.

It is the door to your holy sanctum.

The door to eternal happiness.

If you have any question, ask the diamond.

It holds all the answers.

****

Prana and Emily were both lost in thoughts as they sat on a bench, watching the clouds moving to one side for the full moon to shed its brightness around.

'Now I understand what Rose meant when she said things will get more intense,' said Emily.

'I would get on the next plane back home if I had not met nice people like Rose and you,' joked Prana.

Emily stood up and rubbed her stomach that was aching a bit after her heavy dinner. 'What about Nathan?' she asked.

'He is nice and excellent at helping us relax.'

'What's up between you?' asked Emily, standing in front of Prana, with her hands on her hips.

Prana was puzzled. 'What do you mean?'

'I saw you leaving with him the other day.'

'Oh, he showed me a place for meditation.'

'Come on! Don't tell me that you haven't noticed,' said Emily, impatiently.

'Noticed what?'

'He has a crush on you!'

Prana felt like someone has thrown cold water on her face. 'Stop it, Emily. This is not funny.'

Emily stared at her. 'I'm serious.'

'This can't be true,' said Prana, nervously.

'I'm sorry if I upset you. I thought you would feel pleased about this. He is such a nice guy.'

'I'm just exhausted right now,' said Prana as she stood up.

'Maybe he's the one you need to forget about James,' persisted Emily.

'I can't speed process my feelings. I'm going to bed. We have an early start tomorrow,' replied Prana.

She left, without waiting for Emily this time. She did not want to talk about this. In her heart, she prayed for her friend to be wrong.

****

Dear Diary,

Today reminded me of this beautiful saying, the darkest hour is just before dawn. The sun then shines its light again.

Am I at fault?

Partly, and I take responsibility for it.

Do I deserve happiness?

Only if I make it through the dark hole that keeps coming up.

What is on the other side of the hole?

My inner sanctum. It is waiting for both of us.

And enter with love the temple of your heart.
Heart is the holy sanctum where I reside.
Offer to me the ruby of your mind.
That is the sweetest offering,
A mind that has died.
Give up for good tomorrow, which is false.
Immerse yourself and dwell in the heart instead.

Ramana's song – Kirtana

Chapter 6

2nd Session – Loving your Inner Child

As they sat together, ready for the fifth day of the retreat, there was a mixture of emotions in the Angel Room. The tick tock of the old wooden wall clock sounded like the timer on a bomb about to blow up.

Prana found it simpler to ignore the butterflies going insane in her stomach and instead tried to guess what was going on for the others. She thought Heidi looked agitated, maybe waiting for the bomb to go off in her head. Her hands clasped together, rested on her lap as she kept folding and unfolding her legs. From the corner of her eyes, she noticed Jayan looking spaced out, staring at the clock, as if they were having an intimate conversation. Despite her blue eye shadow, pink blush and cherry lipstick, Emily looked sad. This was unlike her.

The setting was different today with chairs placed in a semi-circle. There were two other chairs facing them three metres away. The small table was in between, covered with pens, paper, and boxes of tissue. Her thoughts were interrupted as Rose walked in, looking even younger than before in her short-sleeved orange cotton kurti and an ankle-long white skirt. She sat on one of the opposite chairs.

'Good morning,' she said with her usual kind smile. '*Loving your Inner Child* is one of my favourite sessions. It is the doorway to self-love in the present time and in the future. It helps us understand how precious our life is and that it is our responsibility to make the best out of it. As you now know, negative beliefs can limit this process. We might find it difficult to believe that our inner child is strong. Today, we will ask for guidance from the angels to help us let go of these beliefs.'

Heidi started sobbing. 'This all feels too hard for me. Since satsang I have been feeling guilty and unloved. I was never close to anyone but at least I knew what to do. My job was my life. Now I don't even know who I am anymore.'

'Heidi, for the time being, let go of needing to know how your life will unfold. I feel that this deconstruction is important for you to find your true self and what you are really meant to do. We will create positive affirmations to help this happen at the right time,' said Rose, handing her some tissues.

After wiping her eyes, Heidi asked. 'How do I let go?'

'Everyone let us start with a guided exercise. Close your eyes, take a nice deep breath in, and let it out. That's it,' said Rose.

'Place your hands in front of you and imagine that you are holding a box. It can be any colour, shape, and size. Now, visualise your thoughts as small clouds moving from your head into the box, one by one ... white clouds, grey clouds, no need to rush ... Put all the clouds of thoughts in the box. Gently, close the lid. Place it to one side and open your eyes.'

Rose waited for them to be ready.

'Love is a universal gift accessible to each one of us at any point in time. All we must do is tap into the consciousness and claim our share. It doesn't matter if you have felt love or not before, we all have an equal share. Aruna is a place where broken hearts and souls can feel loved again. Heidi, please come and sit next to me.'

Heidi moved from the semi-circle to the seat next to Rose.

'What is coming up for you right now honey?' she asked.

'A scene from last year keeps coming up, when my manager told me that I had been sacked. I felt increasingly rejected and alone as I drove back home,' said Heidi, shaking her head in denial. 'Every night I lie in the dark hoping to erase what happened, but the scene persists. I feel the whole world is against me. It gets harder to breathe and the panic starts.'

'Losing your job is not the real problem here. Let's go on a journey to find out if there could be a deeper root cause to your fear,' said Rose in her soothing voice. 'Close your eyes and think of a night when you were lying in the dark in your bedroom. Imagine yourself getting out of bed and walking towards the window. As you open it, the room is flooded with light coming from the sky. An angel appears. He is your guardian angel who will always be by your side. Can you see this happening?'

Heidi's body relaxed as she nodded.

'Would you like to give him, or her, a name?'

'She is Afriel.'

Rose carried on, 'Is there anyone else in the room?'

'There is a yellow nightingale, trapped in a cage. Its eyes are filled with sorrow.'

'You might notice that Afriel has brought a book with her. It is a very special and unique book in which the story of your life is written, from the moment you were born. In your mind's eye, open the book on the page where you had this conversation with the manager.'

'Okay, I am on that page,' said Heidi.

'Now turn the pages backwards. It is safe to look back on your life and check if anything happened previously that made you to feel a similar despair. Afriel is here to help if you feel scared.'

Heidi's brows furrowed in thought. 'I stopped on a page when I was 6 years old. I am in the living room with my father.'

'What is happening?' encouraged Rose.

'I asked if he could buy me a football, but he replied sharply that I am only a girl, and girls are meant to play with dolls. He added that if I was born a boy which was his prayer, he would have bought me balls and cars.'

Heidi choked back on her tears. 'I started crying and dad told me that only weak girls like me cry and that boys are strong. He said if I wanted daddy to be proud of me now, I had to do better things in life and make him honoured. I felt so ashamed to be a girl.'

'You are doing really great Heidi. You have uncovered your core emotion which is shame. What else is coming up here?' asked Rose.

'I grew up believing that I should be as tough as a man. At work, I was the only woman in the team who visited construction sites. I had the biggest clients.'

'Great Heidi, this is a strong unhealthy belief. Is there any other belief?'

'I am unable to have a man in my life as my own energy pushes them away.'

'What else?'

'I work so hard that I don't know how to cope in a relationship.'

'Indeed Heidi, this has turned into the pattern in your life. Anything else?'

'I am scared to live my own life. I just need to be the son my father never had.'

'This is a bit truth you have realised. We will now slowly come back to the where you were in the bedroom, when you got out of the bed and went to the window. In your mind's eye, look around. Has anything changed?' asked Rose.

Heidi looked shocked. 'In the nightingale's eyes I see the six-year-old me! She always felt like a guilty prisoner in her own body.'

'Are you ready to open the cage and set her free? Are you ready to accept her as she is? Are you ready to accept yourself for who you are honey? This is your choice.'

'Absolutely,' replied Heidi with confidence.

'Ask Afriel to take your father's expectations away. Let go of all shame and guilt.'

Heidi's face was glowing.

Rose carried on, 'Visualise Afriel opening the cage door. The nightingale's wings spread as she flies out and transforms into the six-year-old you, your inner child. We will now create your sanctum to welcome her and the present day you.'

Heidi did not need any more guidance. She was the flying nightingale, effortlessly creating her new world. 'We are sitting in my heart, surrounded with a pink light. My inner child is sitting on my lap, and I hold her close to my chest.'

'Perhaps you could give her a gift to become friends again and clear away any shame that might still be hidden in some cells and molecules?'

Heidi's face lit up. 'I gave her a ball! I see the ball rolling through her body, leaving smaller balls in its path. They transform into pacmans who are spreading the pink light everywhere.'

'Is the pink light of any significance?' asked Rose.

Heidi placed her hands on her heart. 'Afriel says that it is the consciousness of universal love, starting from your own heart.'

'This consciousness is now a permanent part of you.'

'Before we end, check with Afriel if he has a message for you from the Universe?'

'He is saying that whenever fear comes, I can wash it away by breathing in this universal love and wrapping the pink light around me,' replied Heidi with a heavenly smile.

'Embrace this light and stay in the love for a moment Heidi,' said Rose. She looked at the others and added, 'We all put our thoughts in a box when we started. Some strong beliefs were hidden in Heidi's box:

I am rejected and alone, I fear spending the rest of my life alone, I feel the world is against me, I feel guilty to be a girl, I should be as tough as a man, I am unable to have a man in my life as my own energy pushes them away, I work so hard that I don't know how to cope in a relationship.'

'*Visualise* yourself opening the box and letting these unhealthy beliefs dissolve in the universal love. Can you replace them with some positive ones?'

Heidi nodded.

'I love myself; I welcome loving people in my life now, I am a part of the Universal love, I am proud to be a woman, I release myself from guilt, I honour every part of who I am, I choose self-love, it's okay to feel vulnerable.'

'Perfect, breathe them in one by one and feel these beliefs integrating and becoming a part of you,' said Rose. 'Keep repeating them every day. Remember them when life challenges come up. Always be proud of yourself.'

'Thank you everyone. I could feel your support,' said Heidi, opening her eyes.

Prana was awed by the peace emanating from Heidi's eyes. She looked like someone new. It was easy to tell that she needed some quiet reflection time as she returned to her seat.

'Who would like to open their box next?' asked Rose.

'Can I give it a try?' asked Emily.

Rose nodded as she pointed to the chair next to her.

Emily made herself as comfortable as possible in the chair that was just wide enough for her hips to fit in. 'The box is heavy, but I don't feel anything.'

'What do you mean?' checked Rose.

'I think that my box is heavy with food not thoughts, but it doesn't disturb me. I look forward to opening it,' answered Emily, genuinely.

'Why do you look a bit sad then?' asked Rose

'I am disappointed with myself. I came here in hope of finding a way to lose weight, instead I eat more, even when I am not hungry,' said Emily, blushing through her make-up.

'Have you noticed the thoughts that come up just before you reach out for extra food? Each thought has a corresponding reaction in the body.'

'In my mind, I tell myself *it's a small piece and it won't make a big difference,* but I do it so many times that by the end of the day it ends up making such a big difference that I sometimes even feel sick.'

'Comfort eating is a way to prevent emotions from coming up. It makes you feel good at the time, but this doesn't last long because you feel guilty for having done it and the feelings that triggered it are still here. Let us check with your inner child where it all started.'

'No, please…' said Emily, anxiously. 'Nothing will come up and I don't want to waste everyone's time. It was a bad idea. I was hoping that you could give me some advice. We don't need to do the whole going back to childhood thing.'

Rose nodded slowly, 'I can certainly give advice, but I need some information to know where to start. All you have to do is relax and look in my eyes ... That's it ... Do you remember a memory around the time when you started eating more?'

'I was around ten years old. At first, the temptation was there usually when I was stressed before exams. Over the years, it turned into a habit which became hard to stop.'

'Were you struggling to get pass marks?' questioned Rose.

Emily explained what happened, with a distant voice, as if she was telling somebody else's story. 'I had average marks and I was not bright like my beautiful sister. She is a year older and always scored the highest marks in her class. My parents expected me to follow in her steps which stressed me out. I started snacking before revising as well as during and after. I did the best I could but failed to meet their expectations. I can still see the disappointment in their eyes when they looked at my results sheet.'

A single tear rolled down Emily's right cheek, followed by a fine line of mascara. 'After two years, my mum said *there's no point trying any harder you will never be as good as your sister. Besides, your extra weight is a bigger concern now. You will soon be too fat to go through the doors.*'

Emily's face turned pale as those words hit her like a punch in the stomach. 'Don't get me wrong,' she added quickly. 'My parents always loved me.'

'I am sure they do, but it doesn't change how their disappointment made you feel. You tried to block it, but at a deeper level, your cells shut down the pain by filling themselves with food. It's time to be honest with yourself … How did your parents' disappointment make you *feel*?' asked Rose, slowly.

Emily broke into tears. ' Both stupid and fat! Fat and stupid!'

Her words came pouring out like a massive confession that had been withheld for years. 'It was a downfall from there on. I put on thirty kilos, and I looked like a monster next to my attractive sister. People always complimented her and hardly noticed me. I felt abandoned to the point of hoping that my parents would still want to fix me, but no one cared about me anymore. Although the love was there, I had been written off as *forever stupid and fat – case closed.* I got used to it and I did not even try to lose weight.'

Rose thought for a moment before asking. 'Why do you suddenly want to lose weight now?'

'I met my boyfriend Kevin last year. He is so handsome that I often wonder how he fell in love with me. I have doubts about his intentions now,' said Emily, sadly.

'You have to remove those unhelpful beliefs that got created when you were younger if you want to have a better understanding of what is happening with Kevin.'

Emily listened attentively.

'You labelled yourself as a closed case, stuffed away in a box, under a stock of food. If you want to lose weight, you need to open the case again and change those beliefs now,' said Rose. 'Take a deep breath in … and let it out.'

Emily closed her eyes again.

Rose guided her. 'Imagine that you are walking in a forest. There are tall trees on both sides. It is very quiet. Not a single leaf is moving. You come to an area where the forest splits into two paths leading in opposite directions. On the left path, you go back to the past where the younger Emily is waiting. On the right one, you go to the future time where you get a clearer picture of how your life will be once you start living more healthily.'

'I can see the paths,' confirmed Emily.

'Good, as you walk to the left, you find the younger Emily, sitting on a bench, with the box next to her. She is holding a page with those lines written on it,' said Rose. '*I am disappointed with myself, I will never be as good as my sister, I fail to meet my parents' expectations, I will always be stupid and fat, I give up trying to lose weight, I am a closed case.*'

'This still feels so real,' said Emily anxiously.

'Don't worry, this is how it's meant to feel. You may now choose a guide to set her free from those beliefs.'

There was some relief in Emily's voice. 'Archangel Raphael is here.'

'Take your time to *feel* how he is helping her,' encouraged Rose.

Emily was half smiling and half serious while the inner conversation took place.

'He told her that she has to destroy what is written on the paper for the box to open. Those beliefs were created from stress in her head and none of it is real. Together, they make a big fire, and she throws the paper in the fire. They watch it burn until there is nothing left but flames of freedom.'

'Excellent Emily. How does the younger you feel?' asked Rose.

'So much better! I have a confession to make. I never had good grades because I was forced to do the same subjects as my sister. I hated economics and maths! I wanted to study literature, but my mother always believed that there was no future in this and pressured me in choosing topics I was not good at. This stressed me.'

'Ah, the truth is now coming out. Thank you for sharing this today.'

'The box is now open, and I take all the food and throw it in the fire as well.'

'Brilliant! Archangel Raphael is now placing his warm hands on top of the head of the younger you. A green healing light emanates from them and flows in her body, all the way down to her feet. It feels soothing. Feel it going into every cell and molecule, and any space in between, clearing her whole being from anything unhealthy that might be left.'

Emily's face was glowing. 'I feel lighter.'

'You can now ask archangel Raphael and the younger you to walk back to the present moment in the forest. See yourself welcoming her with an open heart. Let her know that you love and accept her. Together, you are one,' said Rose, guiding her.

'I also tell her that I am sorry for not believing in her. And, for not protecting her and stuffing her with food instead,' replied Emily with regret.

'Now that you have found each other again, let go of all regrets! Visualise an optimistic future ahead. Archangel Raphael asks you to create new healthy beliefs. Let them come up.'

Emily spoke out the words straightaway, without hesitation. '*It's okay to be different from my sister. I am good just as I am, I choose to be myself, I live up to my own expectations, I change for the better, I have the power to discover my true potential, I love myself, I eat healthily, I honour and respect my body and I take care of my body for myself first.*'

'Beautiful! You may now thank archangel Raphael and ask him for a final piece of advice before letting him go.'

'He is saying: Your body is a temple. Cherish it. Trust your gut feeling and go with what feels right,' replied Emily.

'Beautiful words of wisdom…,' whispered Rose. 'It is now time to come back to this present moment, in the room with all of us. When you are ready, you can open your eyes.'

Emily's eyes were glowing like shining stars in a dark sky. She wrapped her arms around herself and looked around. She was still wearing the same tight dress and her hips were still squashed in the chair, yet she looked graceful.

'I feel exposed,' she whispered.

Rose took her shawl off and wrapped it around Emily's shoulders. 'I am sure that you do … There is a lot shifting going on within you right now. If you look around, you will see something has changed in the others also.'

Emily slowly looked at Heidi, Jayan and Prana.

She felt a close connection with them. She knew a secret part of their lives in the same way that they knew hers now. Secrets that you only share with people you trust.

Rose stood up and stretched. 'Emily, we will wait a few days before going down the right path in the forest and seeing what comes up in your relationship for the future. For the time being, think of your new beliefs before going for meals and choose consciously.'

'I can tell something has definitely shifted,' said Emily.

'Be gentle with yourself for the coming days. Emotions and memories will be coming up. Jayan, while we are on this topic, has anything come up for you since your last session?'

Jayan cleared his throat and loosened his scarf before talking. 'I would like to share with you a list of behavioural patterns that came up.'

'This is the perfect time. Beliefs and behaviour patterns are intertwined,' replied Rose.

'The first belief came up after my mother passed away. It was that *women will always leave me.* These beliefs followed, *I will always feel humiliated, I am a coward, I will never be healthy again, I will die early like my mother.*'

'These are very powerful! Well done for uncovering them,' said Rose.

Jayan carried on, half smiling. 'During my visualisations, these positive ones came up: *I am allowed to express how I feel, I am a man of honour, I choose to have fun and enjoy life, I am healed in every possible way, and I live a love and happy live.*'

'Excellent affirmations. As simple as it sounds, repetition has a powerful effect on the mind. Keep repeating them, let them become part of your whole being,' encouraged Rose.

‘I was looking at the clock earlier and I asked myself the same question as I did many times before, how long do I have left to live?’ said Jayan. ‘It was the only thought that went in my box. I opened it quite easily and found a piece of paper with the answer in it, *you have as long as you choose.*’

Rose smiled. ‘You said it all.’

‘There is a problem though. I still haven’t been able to forgive my wife.’

Jayan cringed as a rush of pain stabbed him like a knife in the throat.

‘As you start letting go of resentment, you will find it easier to forgive. This too shall pass.’

****

Prana felt her nails digging into her palms. It was her turn. She was scared of saying the wrong things.

She felt the heat of shame spreading across her cheeks.

‘I have come to accept that I grew up as a shadow. I find it hard to connect with my inner child. I wonder if she even exists.’

‘From the moment you were born in a physical form, your inner child was created,’ affirmed Rose. ‘You cannot find her because you have been looking outwards all the time. It’s time to turn your attention inwards.’

Prana was restless. ‘My imagination is getting wild. I could feel a presence behind my back earlier when I was holding the box.’

‘Close your eyes and describe to me what you see. Let the words out, no matter how crazy it sounds,’ reassured Rose.

Prana’s words started spilling out like a waterfall. ‘I am standing in front of a mirror. When I look at it, I see a baby. She is lying on the beach, with a cute smile on her face. A massive wave suddenly comes and pulls her into the sea. I am horrified as I watch her disappear. I stand frozen in glue, unable to reach her. I am as useless as a shadow.’

She opened her eyes and started crying in bereavement. She wrapped her arms around herself and started rocking in the chair.

‘I tried to help you, I tried to help you,’ she repeated in despair.

Rose waited for her anguish to dissolve before asking, ‘Who were you trying to help?’

‘Oh my God…. my twin sister,’ said Prana.

‘What happened?’ asked Rose softly.

‘I had forgotten about this until now, but when I around five, I overheard a conversation between my parents. My dad was telling my mum that it would be nice to have another baby. She replied that she did not want one after the trauma she went through when my twin sister died stillborn. It was a serious conversation between them, and I knew I shouldn’t interfere. I asked my neighbour what stillborn meant, and I thought it was my fault. It was the first time that I felt guilt in my life and from that moment onwards, it never left me.’

'What is the first thing that comes to your mind if I ask, what are you guilty about?' asked Rose softly.

'I don't deserve to be alive! Why am I the one who is still here? Why not her?'

'Prana, I felt the same survivor guilt when I lost my family in the car accident. It is this guilt which makes you believe only death can bring you everlasting peace. This is an illusion. Go ahead and end your life if that's what you want. It is the easy way out,' said Rose as if they were talking about the weather.

Her serenity helped Prana calm down.

She added gently, 'However, ask yourself, why has the Universe spared you? What's the intention behind this?'

'I don't know.'

'All revelations are in the dark hole which has been tormenting you. Step into it.'

'You make everything sound easy,' murmured Prana, annoyed.

'It's because I've been there.'

Prana felt nauseous. Nothing made sense anymore.

'I am too exhausted to carry on,' she said.

'Okay darling. This dark hole will not leave you until you dare to step in and face all your life's challenges. But I agree that now might not be the right time. We'll end the session here,' said Rose. 'You all have a good night's rest. You will feel fresh in the morning.'

****

They were floating, close to each other. They looked the same on the outside, yet they were different on the inside. They completed each other until one of them slowly detached herself and floated away in a wave. The other one tried to reach out, but the umbilical cord was too short. She watched helplessly, filled with guilt.

'It was not your fault. I was not ready. I chose to leave, and you chose to live. You cannot be the shadow of someone who never existed. Wake up … Wake up ... Wake up …'

Prana woke up in a sweat. Her heart was racing. The words resonated in her head like thunder. She felt sadness swelling in her chest as she said goodbye to her sister. She cried until her heart felt empty. It was a good empty, one that was waiting to be filled with something fresh.

Thin rays of light peeped through the curtain. Prana got out of bed and went to the balcony. The sun was rising like a new-born, in a clear sky.

She felt a burst of energy in her body as her heart filled with happiness and she smiled.

She stroke her stomach with love. 'Good morning, my baby.'

Where there is laughter, there's God.
Where there is seriousness, there's ego.

H.W.L. Poonja

Chapter 7

A little bit of fun

Emily's head emerged from her bedroom on the fifth knock.

'Good morning dear, are you ready?' asked Prana.

Emily nodded and groaned as they made their way quietly down the staircase. 'These early starts are killing me. Did you have a good night sleep?'

'It started off well, but I'd say not enough. The noisy birds wake me too early,' said Prana with a yawn.

In the courtyard the small group was already assembled, Nathan's tall frame moving between the figures as he greeted them all.

'Hello ladies, everything OK?' he smiled at the pair.

They both pulled a funny face, knowing he was not really expecting an answer but simply pointing to the fact that they were late again.

They followed his lead along the dusty driveway as it narrowed to a well-trodden path. They filtered into a single column of ten, moving silently, save for the soft crunch of footsteps. The cool air was fresh and grew damper as they reached the stream. Prana snuggled deeper into her turtleneck cape and understood now why Nathan had asked everyone to wear long sleeves today. Crossing the footbridge interrupted their rhythm, their feet clattering on the worn wooden planks. It was the first time they had headed in that direction.

'I hope he knows where we're going,' moaned Emily. 'I'm lost already.'

'SShhh!' hissed Prana, who was last in the line. 'Just follow the others.'

As they stepped along the winding path between the trees, the first hint of lightness appeared in the sky. It was still dark, but less oppressively so than in the dead of night. The crunch of their footsteps became a rustle as they made their way across the leaves and twigs that carpeted the ground. Moments later they entered a clearing whose shape and size were unclear in the half-light. Nathan positioned them in rows and took up his place before them. They unrolled their mats and tidied their belongings into neat piles.

'So, lie on your backs and hug your knees into your chest,' he said. 'We'll do a few gentle warm-ups stretches to loosen our limbs. It won't be long before we're feeling good.'

The distant sound of cows mooing synchronised with his voice. Listening closely to his voice Prana followed as best she could. Gradually the sky overhead became grey, then shades of orange and pink washed the night away. The group began the Surya Namaskar series they had been learning all week at the centre.

'*Aha*,' thought Prana, '*this makes more sense now*.'

Nathan had positioned them facing due East, and with impeccable timing had contrived this part of their practice to coincide with the sun's first rays filtering through the trees. His clear voice led them smoothly through the steps.

'Inhale, reaching up. Exhale, folding forwards. Inhale the leg backward, exhale the other leg…'

As their bodies warmed from the exercise Prana felt the sun's early warmth upon her face. Breathing deeply through her nostrils she could feel the crisp forest air filling her lungs mixed with scents of damp earth and leaves, a hint of wild parsley and wood smoke from the village.

Emily was out of breath within twenty minutes. It would probably have been easier if she had worn something looser than her very tight leggings.

'How much longer?' she panted.

'Not very long,' said Nathan. 'You can rest anytime if you need a break.'

She glanced sideways hoping that others were ready to stop. She felt uncomfortable as she observed them moving in perfect synchrony and blamed herself for joining the morning classes only twice. Even Jayan was both relaxed and focused.

'*If he can do it, so can I!*' thought Emily, before taking a deep breath and joined in the next Surya Namaskar.

After ten series, Nathan asked them to put their mats away and stand bare feet in a circle. He joined them, positioning himself between Prana and Heidi.

'We will complete the set with a massage. Turn to the right and place your hands on the shoulders of the person in front of you. Keep your eyes closed and feel your weight sinking in the damp soil,' he instructed as his warm hands covered Prana's shoulders.

She felt her body jolt as his hands pressed into her skin sending a sudden burning sensation in her chest.

Nathan looked around to make sure they were doing it right.

'Gently massage the shoulders,' he continued.

He whispered in Prana's ear, 'Your muscles are rock hard. Relax …. Let them turn to jelly.'

Prana wondering if Emily's assumption had been right all this time. *Had Nathan chosen to stand behind her on purpose? Or was it simply a coincidence that out of ten people, he ended up there?* She was relieved when he moved to the centre of the circle.

'Take a few steps back and leave some space between each other,' he said. 'Then bring your arms down by your side and shake them… Shake your whole body… Imagine yourself shaking off layers of dust.'

At first there were giggles as some of them tried shyly. The whole group was soon playful, especially when Nathan did some silly jumping jacks while chanting *aum*. He pulled out his phone and played a *Ganesha Trance* song.

'Give the child in you permission to awaken, come out and play again! You can shake or dance, with your eyes open or closed. Whatever makes you comfortable.'

Heidi imitated him with the jumping jacks. 'My inner child is awakening!' she said laughing.

The excitement was contagious. Prana and Emily were holding hands and swaying together. Some of the other ladies were singing while dancing.

Jayan was breathless when they stopped. 'My energy is going up and down like a mad yo-yo! This is the best I've felt in years.'

Nathan slowed down gradually and stopped. He waited for all of them to be still again and their breaths to be even.

'Fun is spiritual. Shake your body every day. It helps you get rid of the lethargy that's stuck in places you don't even know, and gets the energy flowing,' he said.

They made their way back to the courtyard like a group of happy bunnies.

Prana felt every cell in her body buzzing with life. She was more than ready to embrace what life had planned for her. She looked up at the blue sky and felt so grateful for the moment she decided to come on this trip.

****

They had been flipping through the pages of their translation pocket books for several days now.

'Hindi must be one of the most difficult languages in the world,' said Prana.

'Thank God most people speak English here,' said Emily.

'We should be fine if we remember the important words, *Namaste* and *Sukriya*.'

Prana's attention was drawn to a movement over Emily's shoulder. 'Look who's here.'

John had just stepped in the courtyard. He was making his way to a bench close to theirs, unaware of their presence.

'The tables have turned!' said Emily.

'What do you mean?'
'It's time for John and me to have a chat.'
'You know that he's not supposed to talk!'
'That's the whole point. Let's give him a taste of his own medicine.'
'Don't be mean,' scolded Prana, in vain.
'Hi John, do you mind if I join you?' said Emily in a friendly tone. 'Oh sorry, I forgot that you're stuck in your own company.'
John was sitting cross-legged and opened a book. He ignored her behind his sunglasses.
'You'll never guess what happened this morning. I had only one masala dosa, a bowl of fruit and two cups of tea at breakfast. No paratha, no lassi. I'm quite proud of myself. That's good progress, don't you think?'
He kept reading or pretended to.
Emily laughed. 'You must be really talented to read a book upside down.'
John put his book down, uncrossed his legs and took his sunglasses off. He stared at her unflinchingly.
'Gosh, if looks could kill, I would be dead by now. You seem to have aged ten years in less than a day. I wonder what you will look like by tomorrow.'
Prana could not help laughing as she overheard the one-way banter. John was not allowed to talk, but no one said he that could not murder someone. She joined them and grabbed Emily's arm.
'OK, that's enough. Let's go,' she said.
Emily gave John an innocent angel smile. 'Oh no, did I offend you? If you'll excuse me now, I have a busy day with better things to do that talking to an old self-centred person.'
Prana dragged her away, both laughing like happy kids.

It had been easy to find some time alone with Nathan. Prana arranged to accompany him on his next trip to collect milk from the farm. Just the two of them. She had to find out if he was interested in her, but she was nervous if it happening to be the case. While waiting for him, she wandered in the outdoor prayer area, admiring the fascinating statues. It had amazed her from the very first day that Aruna retreat held a combination of spirituality and religion. They blended in naturally and guests could decide for themselves which path they chose.
She had read about the stories of the deities and was particularly captivated by Mother *Durga*. The goddess wore red clothes and sat on what was either a lion or a tiger. She carried weapons and a lotus flower in her ten hands. Durga was depicted as invincible and used her divine feminine energy to protect her devotees from evil. She was worshipped for bringing freedom from pain and suffering.

'This must be the reason I feel relief each time I see her statue. If I succeed in finding my own feminine power, I will set myself free from pain,' thought Prana.

Nathan made his way towards her nonchalantly. Prana had been so used to seeing the yoga instructor in plain kurtas every morning that he looked strange wearing a pair of blue shorts and beige t-shirt with the *aum* symbol printed in black. He tilted his straw hat on the side to greet her as he caught her eyes. She did not understand why her knees got shaky. Her body seemed to have a mind of its own lately.

'Are you ready?' asked Nathan, bringing her back to reality.

Prana nodded.

She had not yet explored this side of the retreat. The dry and flat footpath leading to the farm contrasted with the damp clearing. Prana was glad that she had a shawl to protect her head from the afternoon sun. Patches of small colourful blooms, lilies, tulips, roses, and chrysanthemums grew in the garden. Thick metre-high bushes grew between the garden and the wall that stood between the retreat and the road. Pink bougainvillea plants climbed elegantly, hiding the white wall. A handful of monks were attending to clipping the lilies and thinning the bougainvillea bushes. Prana slowed down and watched them.

Looking over his shoulder, Nathan said, 'You're so quiet, that for a moment I thought I'd lost you.'

'I am blown away by the monks. The first time I saw them they were meditating, the second time they were laughing like mad in the church and today they are working under the sun like dedicated gardeners. I am stunned at how they look perfect at whatever they do,' commented Prana.

Nathan gestured towards one of the monks. 'Their technique is simple. Focus. Look at his eyes. What do you see in them?'

Prana frowned. 'What do you mean? He is just looking at the plant while pulling out dead leaves.'

'That's the secret. He is not *just looking* but putting all his attention on what he is doing in this present moment and whatever he does flows easily. He is not distracted by us.'

'Why do monks choose to stay single?' asked Prana as they carried on walking.

'Love comes with attachment which often causes anger, jealousy, resentment ... the list is long. It is easier to progress spiritually when you have a clear path.'

'Have you chosen the path of yoga teaching to become one of them?'

Nathan shook his head. 'I certainly want to progress on my spiritual path, but I would like to do this alongside someone with the same vision.'

'Have you found your life partner?' asked Prana, trying not to sound too interested in his answer.

Nathan stopped and looked at her, 'Interesting question... I am not in a relationship but it's possible that I might have found someone, and we have not recognised each other yet. It's too soon for me to answer your question until she recognises me.'

'I hope the answer you seek will come soon,' said Prana as they carried on. *Oh God, why did his reply have to be so complicated,* she thought, even more confused.

The calming scent was soon replaced with the rural smell of cow dung as they approached the farm.

A small herd of various shades of brown cows was grazing on the tired grass. It struck Prana how healthy they looked compared to the withered ones that she saw in Delhi. The farmer was cleaning the shed and singing so loud that Prana felt sorry for the cows, especially the one who was tied to a wooden frame close to the farmer, quietly munching on a heap of hay.

'Namaste,' he shouted as they got close.

'Namaste Pappu,' Nathan shouted back.

Pappu looked small, dirty, and happy, standing next to the clean brown cow. He patted her back and bellowed, 'Me go get milk.'

'I forgot to mention that Pappu is deaf,' said Nathan after he left.

'I kind of guessed,' replied Prana as she stroked the cow's back. 'She's beautiful.'

A copper bell was hanging to the collar that she wore around her neck, with her name Devi engraved in it. Her skin was polished. Prana giggled as Devi sniffed her hair.

'Be careful,' said Nathan but it was too late.

Prana jumped in horror when Devi unexpectedly stuck her drooling tongue out and licked her cheek.

'Aaahhhhh!' she screamed.

She stepped back, straight into Nathan's arms. Prana felt his hard chest muscles pressing against her back through her thin clothes. Although she enjoyed the sensation, it caught her by surprise, and she pulled away. She wiped her wet flushed cheek with her scarf, hoping that he could not hear her pounding heartbeat.

Pappu was back holding a crate loaded with ten bottles of fresh milk. He asked Prana something in Hindi.

'Would you like to milk Devi? Just for a bit of fun?' translated Nathan.

'*Haan*! Yes!' bellowed Prana enthusiastically.

'It is as not easy as it may look,' he warned.

'Sit,' Pappu told her, pointing to the stool next to the cow.

She watched carefully as the little man held the two front teats of the udder. He wrapped a thumb and forefinger around each teat and gently squeezed them to remove any dust. Once satisfied, he nodded to himself. He pulled them downwards as Prana observed attentively.

'Down. Down. OK?' he checked with her.

Prana rolled up her sleeves.

'*Haan,*' she confirmed.

'This feels so strange,' she said as the warm teats filled her palms.

She squeezed but only a few drops came out.

Pappu threw his arms up in disapproval. 'Down.'

The milk began to come out in a thin stream when she squeezed and pulled at the same time. Prana pulled faster as she got the hang of it.

'It's more tiring on the arms than I expected,' she said.

'I told you so,' said Nathan, peeping over her shoulder to have a better look.

'You must be an expert at this now?' asked Prana.

She turned to look at him and accidentally twisted the teat at a wrong angle. A splash of milk landed on Nathan's face. He looked perplexed for a second but joined in when the others laughed at him.

Prana passed him her shawl. 'I'm terribly sorry!'

'You don't sound sorry at all,' he replied.

Prana raised an eyebrow when Pappu asked him something and both men started laughing cheekily when he replied.

'He asked if you are my girlfriend,' said Nathan.

'What did you say?' she asked.

'I told him *not yet,* but I'm working on it.'

Wiping her hands, Prana asked, 'Are you ever serious?'

Pappu yelled something once more.

Nathan cleared his throat as if to make a special announcement. 'He seems to think that we would make a nice couple.'

He waited for her to comment but Pappu saved her by saying goodbye as he went back to cleaning the shed.

They chose a shorter path on their way back to the canteen.

After they dropped off the milk, Nathan murmured, 'I am going to the shop to buy a beaded bracelet. Would you like to come? You have probably seen my friend Pooja around. It's a gift for her son,' he added. 'She bakes the most savoury pastries and sweet cakes for the temple. She comes every morning for her deliveries.'

'Oh yes! She's very beautiful.'

They bent to get in through the low door frame of the cottage. Surprisingly, it was high and spacious inside. Tall statues and crystals were placed on the floor. There were two round tables next to each other in the centre of the room. Rows of shelves were nailed to the side walls. Prana looked at the stacked shelves, unsure where to start. The two sellers reminded her of Snow White's dwarfs, Sleepy and Happy. Sleepy who was slowly putting together *malas* did not even raise his head. Happy rushed to them within seconds.

'How can I help?' he smiled.

'I am looking for a Mother Durga statue,' said Prana.

'Please follow me, we have quite a few of them on this shelf,' replied Happy.

Out of the dozens on display, Prana spotted the one calling to her straightaway. It was outstanding with finely carved features, stunning deep colours, and the right medium size to fit in her suitcase.

'I would like to buy this one please,' she said.

Happy smiled and went to pack the statue. Nathan joined them and handed him a bracelet to pack as well.

Prana admired the impressive crystals. Several bowls were aligned on the shelves, each one containing a particular type of stone, including hand stones, eggs, spheres, tumble stones, pendulums, heart shaped ones, standing towers and raw natural styles.

'They are all well-known for their healing properties, especially these ones,' said Nathan. He pointed at the ones labelled amethyst, citrine, jade, sapphire, emerald, rose quartz and onyx.

'This place is a treasure box!' she said, moving to the jewellery area. She unhooked a pair of pear-shaped amethyst earrings and placed it in front of her ear as she looked in a mirror.

'They suit you so beautifully,' said Nathan.

Prana put them back. 'I love them, but they are expensive.'

Happy was back with their wrapped boxes.

'So, what do you think?' asked Nathan casually when they stepped outside.

'About what?' she asked, though she knew what was coming.

'Would we make a nice couple?'

Prana stared at him in distress. 'I can't even imagine being in a new relationship after what I've been through recently.'

Nathan quickly said, 'Please accept my apologies, it was inappropriate of me to ask this. This thought only crossed my mind because of Pappu's comment. Our paths are very different.'

Prana released a sigh of relief and ignored the inexplicable pang of sadness in her heart. At least she got a clear reply now.

'We can still be great friends and keep in touch after you leave,' he added cheerfully, trying to make up for his misstep.

As Prana looked at him, it crossed her mind that he would make a good monk. His eyes revealed no expression.

'You might change your mind once you know everything about me. Would you like to sit in the garden for a talk?' she said.

'Not right now. I need to prepare for the next yoga class. Perhaps another time.'

Nathan turned and left before she could see the pain that he could not hide any longer in his eyes.

Piglet noticed that even though he had a Very Small Heart,
it could hold a rather large amount of Gratitude.

A.A. Milne

Chapter 8

Embracing Gratitude in your Heart Satsang

'If all beings on earth could feel gratitude, no matter what, we would be surrounded with mountains and oceans of love.'

The forty guests, including Aryaji, took a few minutes to meditate on these words written on the whiteboard. Prana and Emily had arrived fifteen minutes before the start time to get a seat in the front row.

After his usual throat-clearing moment, the master said: 'Experiences that we wish never happened bring up emotions we might not even know existed within us until then. In such moments, gratitude might be the last thing that we feel. It's more likely we feel hatred, jealousy, resentment, rage, or despair. When these emotions arise, let them be as intense as they want to, in the same way that you would for happiness. Welcome them as gifts with an open heart.'

'Why? This is like letting enemies in the sanctuary that I have been creating with so much love and care,' said a woman.

'Correct, and they have the right to be there. It is their sanctuary as well. To heal completely, you must stop pretending that it doesn't hurt. Be willing to have your heart broken again and again. Allow the waves of pain in, until you have learnt your lesson. They eventually calm down if you don't react. Simply welcome the pain and observe. They will get bored with nothing to do and leave eventually, like unwelcomed guests.'

Aryaji slowly pushed the space in the air back and forth with his left hand to show what he meant.

'If you push them away, they will fight to stay. They will turn into bigger waves and take up more residence in your life. They will enjoy it as you are giving them a purpose. You might think that you've done a great job if you manage to get rid of them, but they will come back through the windows of your mind when you are off guard, stronger than before. It turns into a vicious circle upsetting everything left, right and centre. You can break the circle by finding gratitude in your heart for the positive things in your life.'

The room was quiet as the small crowd allowed the words to sink in. From the look on some faces, it was easy to tell that they were questioning the advice. It did not take long for a 'but question' to come up.

A woman named Chloe raised her hand. 'This is a beautiful theory, but I have been going through a divorce for a year now and it's difficult for me to find gratitude. I lost my husband, my home, my business, and I started feeling depressed. I am now living in a shared house with five strangers, I started a new job which drains my energy, but I need to earn a salary to pay my rent and feed myself. I feel lonely and I have no time nor inclination to make friends in the new area where I have relocated. This divorce has been dragging on for so long, I feel drained. I don't recognise who I used to be anymore. And you want me to feel gratitude? For what? To whom? I have come here in the hope to find the joy to live again.'

'Thank you for sharing, Chloe. I can sense this falling apart is important for the creation of a new you. Can you embrace it as a transition phase and be patient for what might be showing up next? Gratitude is an integral part of enlightenment. It will be tested, especially for those who have come to this temple. It takes time and effort to accept some situations, but when there will be nothing left to fall apart, when you hit rock bottom, you can only rise again. When you see your glass as half full instead of half empty, your inner sanctum will fill up with self-love once more. Everything is welcome in love and offers you an opportunity to find appreciation. You might find that your divorce was meant to make you move to a new area where your quality of life eventually improves. There might be something new coming your way here. Be open to discovery. Stop fighting the challenges and welcome them in your sanctuary. Welcome the waves of the divorce, new job, depression, let everything in. Just be the observer.'

'But why do I have all these additional difficulties? I don't deserve the additional problems from my husband and the court lost the divorce papers. The new job is ...'

'Stop… Enough Chloe. They are not the problems,' said Aryaji. 'The problem is your mind that does not know how to stop the circle. Remember, what you resist persist. When I look at you, I see a field of possibilities coming up whereas, you see them as issues. For now, what if you could welcome the way these difficulties make you feel? Feel the pain. Sit with it as if you had your best friend here. Once you've made peace with it, see what happens next. You might notice that the whole synchronicity of your life game changes.'

Chloe took a deep breath in and breathed out. 'I see what you mean. I have always been restless person. I think it comes from my mother always putting pressure on me and setting high expectations. She always pointed out on what did not work in my life rather than praising me when I achieved something good. That's why when problems come my way, I can't help feeling like a failure. Even now she makes me feel like I should be ashamed of my divorce.'

'This is your life decision. You have nothing to be ashamed of. Your mother has her own path to live, she can't choose to live yours as well. It's for you to decide where to set your boundaries Chloe. I can tell by looking at you that you are already on the right path. Keep going. Even if you are not sure at first whether you are taking the right way, you know that staying where you would be the wrong thing. So, it is more important to take the risk and get out of your current situation rather than remain stagnant. If you are not heading the right way, you will get the signs to adjust as you go. Just know that all these tests come your way because you have the strength to handle them. It's time to awaken your inner power and handle the problems. Do not fear your own power. Step out there and do to what you believe is your highest potential.'

'I will work on changing this Aryaji,' said Chloe.

'When I look in your eyes Chloe, a saying comes to my mind. *They whispered to her, You cannot withstand the Storm. I am the Storm, she whispered back*. If you meditate on this situation for a bit longer dear one, you might even start to feel grateful to the Universe for having sent souls like your mother and ex-husband into your life to provide you with such heart-opening experiences. Without them, you would not be going through those emotions which would make you question your life to such an extent. Set your focus and intention, then let go. You might want to do some walking meditations along the pathways we have surrounding the gardens. It is quite natural for the mind to wander but keep your attention in the sensations of your steps. See where it takes you.'

Chloe had tears in her eyes. 'I would not have thought of feeling grateful towards my ex-husband, but you have changed my perspective. I certainly need some time to sit with this thought. I will follow your advice about the walking meditations. Please tell us about a significant experience in your life for which you are grateful.'

The guru placed a couple of cushions behind his back and leaned back in his sofa. 'I still remember clearly how it happened twenty-five years ago. Back then, I was a teacher in a secondary school in Mumbai and I led a simple life. I was only slightly intrigued by spirituality, and I meditated for fifteen minutes in the morning. One day, I was waiting at the airport for my flight that had been delayed. After an hour, there was an announcement to inform passengers that we would now be leaving from another gate.'

He bent forward in his chair and lowered his voice, to create more anticipation.

'Soon after the plane took off, I realised that I had left my laptop in the lounge! I felt distressed during the flight. When I reached Delhi airport, they made a call to Mumbai airport to check if my laptop bag was still there, but sadly as expected it had disappeared by then. My distress got worse in the following weeks.'

Perplexed, some people in the room looked at each other.

'Huh … Is that it?' asked Emily.

Aryaji burst out laughing. 'I'm afraid so. What were you expecting? Something more exciting such as I was saved from a plane crash by missing my flight and flying on the other plane?'

There were a few disappointed grumbles.

Emily pursed her strawberry-painted lips. 'There's nothing very life-changing in losing a laptop.'

'This laptop was an important part of my daily life as I was a movie addict back then. It was the only device that I had to watch movies after my working hours. I couldn't afford to buy another one. They were expensive, and I had a mortgage to pay.'

'Please explain the connection with gratitude?' asked a man from the back of the room.

'Suddenly, I had too much time on my hands and shifted my attention to meditate in the evenings by listening to soothing music on the radio. This was how I discovered a deeper part of me which I didn't even know existed until then. It was the start of my journey to create this place where we are all gathered today. Losing my laptop was the seed from where Aruna grew.'

'Incredible,' murmured Emily, in admiration.

'We don't need achievements that impress other people for our lives to change. You can make a big change in the world by showing kindness to someone in need. Personal small changes can turn big one day, if you look after a seed you sow today, then it will become a tree.'

These words resonated with Prana who seized this opportunity to ask, 'What if you are grateful for a personal change but you can't express it because other people will judge you negatively? You don't know if their reactions will make you regret having been grateful in the first place.'

'So long as the reason behind your gratitude is not harming anyone else, there is no need to hide it. Don't let other's judgement affect your life-changing decisions. You will know in your own heart if what you are doing is right. You are your own teacher, you don't need anybody else's validation,' said Aryaji, supportively.

'How will I know if I am grateful for the wrong reason?' Prana pressed.

'It won't take long before you know it as the gratitude won't expand.'

'But, what if others …'

Aryaji raised his hand to stop her. 'Your questioning mind is full of *buts* and *what ifs*. This is a wonderful opportunity for you to go deeper within where the answers will be revealed.'

Prana said nothing. She knew that the answers were already with her, waiting to be let out of the closet. They had been knocking on the door, getting louder every day, since she had arrived at Aruna.

'I know, but maybe I am not ready to hear the answers yet,' she said.

The master looked at her with tenderness. 'Then, take your time, young one. One thing that I always tell people is don't move until The Universe moves you. If you don't feel ready, then there is no rush. Be gentle with yourself.'

Prana felt her body relax and she smiled. 'Thank you Aryaji. This is just what I needed to hear. What are you most grateful for today?'

He looked at them with humility. 'For all of you. My guests are my reason to be in this world. I wake up feeling blessed with your presence, and at night, I go to bed with a heart full of gratitude for the magical moments you bring to Aruna. Guests come and go, but the energy that we share stays forever. It is a permanent contribution. You might see me as different because I am always on this side of the room, but as the poet Hafiz said, *I am just a hole in the flute. My role is to serve as an instrument that holds us together as our paths head in the same direction.*'

The energy shifted in the room as Aryaji bowed his head with a namaste to thank everyone.

'Learn to bring your attention to small things which deserve gratitude, but that are usually overlooked because they are so small. I was deeply touched by an experience that a woman shared recently,' he added. 'She was sitting in a park, worrying over the number of things that she had to do. She had been overwhelmed over the past weeks by the number of things she had to do at home with her three kids and her own job. Then she saw a family arrive for their picnic. There was young disabled girl in a wheelchair. Her mum helped her sit on the bench, and bent down to remove her shoes, before placing her feet flat on the grass. The girl's eyes lit with a childlike excitement.'

'While watching her, the woman felt a weight being lifted from her shoulders. She started to imagine what her life would be if she was unable to do her simple morning rituals, such as get out of bed by herself, making breakfast for the family, shower, get dressed and take the kids to school. She realised how it would be even worse if she had to look after her two kids, the way this mother was doing across the park. She left the park with a grateful heart, looking forward to the tasks awaiting her. This is when perception changes and your cup is half full of opportunities.'

Jayan commented, 'Listening to you, I feel my gratitude growing for the occasional moments when I felt free from pain since I've been here. I notice that painless moments where I can talk for longer, are more frequent now.'

'I am very happy to hear this. A good sign of progress, Jayan! Keep trusting that your healing is happening, and the more you feel grateful for it, the faster you will rise like a phoenix from burnt ashes.'

'How can I make it more frequent?' asked Jayan.

'First, make a list of everything that you can do for yourself,' advised Aryaji. 'Second, take time to notice your natural gifts, such as your energy, your senses, your body. When you catch yourself laughing, ask yourself, what made you laugh? Take the time to be grateful for the beautiful flowers we have outside. Have you been on a morning walk, listened to the birds and breathed in the various natural scents out there? Write down the names of people who you are grateful to have in your life and in what way they contribute to your wellbeing. As you cultivate the habit, it comes more naturally. Another good method is by using your own benefits to help other people in need.'

'I can already tell that I will enjoy this homework,' thanked Jayan.

Aryaji gently moved on, 'Our world has been through a lot of emotional and physical traumas over the past years with the Covid virus. We've been walking around wearing face masks, or keeping social distancing from each other, creating anti-social behaviours that have isolated us for so long that we don't recognise ourselves anymore. What's even worse, we feel awkward to interact with others, even our close ones. At Aruna temple, some of you have spent over a week together already, getting to know each other as a community and others are already from the local village.'

He paused and looked around. 'How about sharing a gratitude hug with the person next to you? Decide who will speak first and then you can swap. Looking at your partner in the eyes, let them know how grateful you are to have met them. In your own words, tell them that they are a special being and play an important role in the world. And then you can give each other a hug.'

There was not a single moment of hesitation among the small group. Words could be heard loud and truthful. Those receiving the words had tears of pure joy in their eyes.

'Feel free to walk around and hug anyone, expressing your gratitude and letting them know you are happy to have met them,' said Aryaji.

The room turned into a joyful kindergarten with chairs being moved around as they embraced each other. It got noisier and happier as the hugs increased. Aryaji made his way down and joined in. It looked like one big hug as they all surrounded him.

Someone softly drew Prana out of the group. She was hypnotised, looking into those intense blue eyes.

'Sorry for the other day. I am grateful that we met, and you are special to me. I mean it without any second intention,' said Nathan kindly.

'I am grateful too,' she replied, feeling her heartbeat going wild already.

It felt magical as Nathan's arms wrapped around her into a big warm hug. Prana did not want to pull away, so she relaxed and enjoyed the moment with her head resting on his shoulder.

****

Prana wished she had come up with some excuse, as she half reluctantly, half keenly, followed Nathan and Emily to the village. She felt exhausted after her morning sickness, but she wanted to get a glimpse of native life. Although Aruna was uphill, from the distance it was hard to make out how the village looked, except for beds, chairs and laundry lines covered with colourful clothes on the rooftops. At night, the illuminated streets and fireworks were visible from her bedroom. They had waited until early afternoon when the cool breeze started blowing to set off. Nathan had tactfully convinced Emily to wear a skirt long enough to cover her knees and a decent top with sleeves. The taxi was waiting when they met near the reception area. It was a short drive to the village.

'This feels like being part of a movie!' exclaimed Prana as they got off at the local market and made their way through the crowd.

Handicraft sellers were walking around with painted scarves, woven fabric handbags hanging on their arms and necklaces dangling along their forearms. Some of them looked funny with a heap of hats pilled on their heads, threatening to tumble with each step. Prana pulled Emily away as she was about to reach out and daringly grab a hat. Juice vendors shouted to catch their attention.

Nathan signalled them to follow him down the hawkers' lane. The left side was packed with vegetable vendors. The stalls were aligned so close together that sellers had to go under them to get in and out. Green and red peppers were shining next to purple aubergines. Baskets of red tomatoes and long green beans surrounded heaps of pale cauliflowers and bitter gourds. Some stalls were green with fresh chilli, packs of various types of lettuces, fresh coriander leaves and spring onion.

Resilient vegetables such as potatoes, onions and pumpkins were stacked directly on the ground at the far end. Vendors shouted their prices, each one trying to be louder than the other and buyers called for discounts. It was funny to watch them walk away slowly, waiting for the vendor to call them back with a better offer.

'But the sellers will hardly earn anything,' remarked Prana.

Nathan laughed. 'No chance of this happening. The displayed prices are double what sellers hope to earn. It's a win-win situation.'
'Surely the people know this,' said Emily.
'Yes, it's an old trick but it works for both sides,' confirmed Nathan.

The next section was packed with fruits, but quieter as the vendors were not competing. Each one sold only one type of fruit. Bunches of bananas, glistening red apples, mangoes, coconuts, oranges, and round watermelons had been carefully aligned on separate stands. Slices of fruit were available in front of each stand for people who wished to taste before buying.
Spice vendors were jammed at the end of the market with mountains of mustard powder, cinnamon, cardamon, dried red chilli, pepper and many more. The air was filled with distinctive aromas that tickled the nostrils. It was obvious straightaway that business was not as popular in this section. Sellers were lazily chewing on spicy *pans* with bored eyes.
As they stepped out of the market, they saw unlucky hawkers who did not have a stall walking around pushing wooden trolleys of both raw and cooked food, followed by diligent flies. A seller made his way towards them, pushing a heavy-looking trolley.
'Coconut? Coconut?' he asked.
Prana almost threw up from his breath that reeked of *pan*.
Nathan reassured the girls. 'Coconut water is very refreshing. You can drink straight from the coconut shell with a clean straw.'
Before they had time to answer, the vendor handed them a shell each.
'Delicious, just what I needed today,' said Prana as she took her first sip.
They exited onto a street where a group of happy children were playing cricket watched over by a couple of elderly men who were sitting under a tree, listening to a blaring radio.

Pooja was busy hanging her laundry in the front garden when they arrived. She looked slim in her light pink cotton saree. Her long black hair was neatly braided and hung down her lean back. The silver bangles clanged as she bent to reach for the wooden pegs. She turned her head at the squeaky sound of the gate opening.
'Welcome,' she greeted them with a beautiful smile. She had a delicate face and warm brown eyes. She could easily pass as a model.
Prana liked her straightaway. There was a calmness and warmth about Pooja that made her feel comfortable. After Nathan introduced them, they followed her inside. The house was simple but held a welcoming energy.
'Please make yourself at home,' she said, nodding towards the couches covered with embroided cushions. There was a low table in the middle covered with small plates, mugs, teaspoons, a bowl of white sugar and napkins. She left the living room and was soon back with a tray covered with bowls of onion pakoras, vegetable samosas, and a steaming teapot.

'I am so pleased that Nathan brought you here. It is rare that I get to practise my English,' she said with a lovely Hindi accent.

'It is rare that I see such delicious savoury food. This smells so fantastic,' said Emily, as she started serving herself.

'You won't find anyone else who makes these first-class pakoras that melt in the mouth! And this Indian tea with some secret spices, I could drink the whole pot,' praised Nathan with a wide grin.

Pooja blushed, 'Nathan is always good at giving compliments.'

'Where is my six-year-old man?' asked Nathan.

'Manu is playing in his bedroom,' she said.

Nathan stood up with his cup of tea. 'If you'll excuse me ladies, I'll leave you to chat while I go and find him.'

Time passed quickly as Pooja told them more about the village and how Rishikesh changed her life.

'If you don't mind me asking, how did you learn such a perfect English?' asked Prana.

'I am originally from Mumbai where I learnt English in high school. It remained part of my daily life when I worked as a secretary,' she explained.

Surprised, Emily said, 'Why did you move here? Mumbai is an awesome city.'

Pooja nodded as if she was expecting this question. 'I met my husband Raju seven years ago, when he came to Mumbai for work. We got closer but we both knew that it would be difficult to carry on as he would soon return to Rishikesh. Still, he proposed to me, and I didn't have to think twice before accepting. He warned me that I might find it hard to settle in a village, on the outskirts of Rishikesh, but my heart had already decided.'

'Was it difficult?' asked Prana.

'I was homesick for months. I was so in love that there were things I hadn't thought about until I got here. Hardly anyone spoke English in my daily life. I had to put away my nice clothes as I could not use them here. I missed my previous job, going to the gym and earning a salary. I started spending more time in the kitchen and doing household chores. Basically, I turned into a housewife, and I was losing my sense of motivation for life.'

'Did you regret your choice?' asked Emily.

'I've had lonely moments until I started my baking job for Aruna. My parents think what I do is simply cooking, but I consider myself a lot more. I am now a self-employed woman, a wife, and a mother,' replied Pooja with a beautiful smile. 'Every morning, I am grateful to wake up with Raju by my side. Life got better when Manu was born. He has brought so much joy to our lives.'

No sooner had she said this that Nathan walked in, carrying a brown-skinned little boy with the happiest eyes in the world. He looked cute in his white batman t-shirt and blue shorts.

'Awww, he's adorable,' said Prana.

Manu made gargled noises and clumsily flapped his left arm to show them his bracelet made of sand-coloured wooden beads. When Nathan put him on the floor, he held onto the table and slowly limped towards Pooja. He leaned against her and placed his arm on her lap.

'Beuh beuh beuh,' he said, shaking the bracelet.

'What a beautiful gift *chacha* Nathan bought you! Did you thank him?' asked Pooja. She raised his hand, admiring the bracelet.

Prana and Emily watched quietly.

'Show your new aunties the bracelet,' said Pooja, pointing at them. 'Go Manu. Show aunties Prana and Emily … the bracelet.'

He held onto the edge of the couch and slowly walked towards them, limping with every step. He stopped in front of Prana and looked at her with a huge smile. She raised him and held him on her lap.

'Manu has cerebral palsy.' explained Pooja. 'We found out when he was two years old that he would never be able to walk properly and that his learning process will be slow.'

Emily had tears in her eyes. 'I'm so sorry about this.'

'Don't be,' replied Pooja softly. 'We love him the way he came to this Earth, our happy little angel. We don't pray for God to change him, but to ease his pain. He is our biggest teacher.'

'In what way?' asked Prana. She stroked Manu's back while he fiddled with her watch.

'He taught me acceptance and gratitude. He taught me to see the good in things that seem wrong. When I struggle with anything, his laughter is enough to make me face the world. I see God in him.'

'I see what you mean. He is a strong little boy,' said Prana. She kissed him on the forehead.

'You would make a very loving mother,' said Pooja.

Prana was taken aback by her comment. 'What makes you say this?' she asked, her heart beating fast.

'I can see it in the way you hold Manu. There is so much love and protection in your embrace. It's a natural part of you.'

'Thank you,' said Prana.

She reluctantly passed Manu to Emily who was waiting with a huge smile and her arms wide open.

'Manu is a fighter. When he falls, very often he stands up again on his own,' said Pooja.

After a few hours of relaxed conversation and playing with Manu, they left having made a new friend in Pooja. Prana knew she had been given a sign from God to make the most of her life as it was offered to her. What she thought to be problems turned into a paper tiger now that she had met little Manu.

****

As expected, she found Rose sitting on her favourite bench in the garden.

'Well honey, come and join me,' she said as Prana approached. 'What has changed?'

Prana raised her eyebrows. 'How can you tell?'

'Your energy has shifted. It's the first time that I see you walk, holding your head higher and shoulders straight. I could smell the confidence from a distance.'

Prana could not help laughing. 'I met a very young teacher. No words were needed for him to show me that I can choose to be happy anytime by accepting myself as I am.'

'Is it Manu by any chance?'

'Is there anything that you don't know?' said Prana, slightly annoyed.

Rose shrugged. 'Some things are slightly easier to guess, honey.'

They looked at each other in the eyes.

In an instant, Prana realised that Rose already knew what she wanted to share.

'I am pregnant,' she said calmly.

She was surprised that was so effortless to get it off her chest, without that immense feeling of guilt that had been eating her from inside for months.

Rose said warmly, 'I am pleased for you baby. I wondered how much longer it would take for you to tell me.'

'When did you guess that one out?' asked Prana.

'The very first day, when we met on the train. You had your hands on your tummy a few times. Behind your tears, there was a mixture of hidden love and pain that spoke for itself,' replied Rose.

'I feel so grateful to be here. Aruna has brought amazing teachers in my life. I feel so ready for a fresh start. I have no idea where I am heading in life, but I know for sure now that my baby is also a teacher in my life,' affirmed Prana.

Rose uncrossed her legs and signalled her to sit in the same position, before saying, 'Very well. Close your eyes then.'

Prana took a deep breath and leaned her back against the bench.

'Some time back, you met an angel who gave you a treasure box. There was a precious mirror inside. Did you keep it?' asked Rose.

Prana nodded.

'Great. Today, take your time and once more try to raise the mirror all the way up to your face,' said Rose.

Prana's face beamed. 'I can raise it this time. The mirror is lighter. I see a beautiful pink light surrounding my face and shoulders. Durga *ma* is standing behind me, supporting me with her strength. My face is shining with love and happiness.'

'Beautiful. Ask Durga *ma* why the mirror felt heavy last time,' asked Rose.

'She is saying that it had always been light. The handle is made of a silver-painted plastic. I was focusing on its appearance which made me believe it was steel,' replied Prana.

'What has changed today?' said Rose.

'I raised the mirror with confidence this time, ready to see myself. I have chosen to let go of others judgement. It doesn't matter what others think or say. This is my life. I am worthy of love. I am my own teacher, and it is my choice how to live my life. I choose pure joy on this earth.'

'You passed your test, sweetheart,' said Rose. 'You can now open your eyes and I suggest that you spend the rest of the evening in silence. Take the time to meditate and allow moments of gratitude to come up. Put pen to paper and see what gets revealed.'

****

Words flowed in her diary and pages turned as Prana made her gratitude list. Unexpected sentences took shape: gratitude for a new life, for giving herself permission to love again, for all the tests that came her way and even for those that were yet to come. She completed it with her gratitude for being given the chance to spend more time with Manu. Pooja had appreciatively taken up her offer to teach Manu some drawing and writing.

'There is one thing remaining,' she said to herself.

Prana stood in front of the ghost mirror on the wall. She had covered it with a towel on the day that she came, as she could not bear looking at herself anymore. She dropped the towel on the floor and slowly removed her clothes, enjoying every single movement.

'I am worthy of love. I love and accept myself, every part of me,' she said as she looked in her own eyes. She lay on the bed and gently caressed her body. The touch of her own hands on her skin after such a long time felt divine. The shame of living in disapproval melted like ice in the sun as she accepted every part of herself.

True forgiveness is one of the most healing, releasing and freeing gifts
that we give to ourselves.
A life full of open forgiveness is a life of Grace.

Brandon Bays

Chapter 9

3rd Session – Finding the Power to Forgive

The Angel Room welcomed them with candlelight and lavender-scented oil that burnt at the centre of a rose quartz crystal. Rose had already taken a seat in the small circle of chairs and closed her eyes while the guests settled and closed the circle around her. Everyone had been feeling emotionally raw since they worked on the gratitude exercises. Emily looked like a new person, and fresh, with no makeup on. She had tied her black and orange curls back in a knot. Although they all felt close to Rose, it was intimidating to be an intimate group of five. They were a smaller group of fifteen staying in the temple now, and some of the others were having their own private yoga or meditation sessions or had gone for walks.

Rose could be both gentle or sharp, depending on what was coming up during the meeting. Right now, she was on the gentle side with a kind smile.

'You might have regrets over things you've said that you wish you could take back, or choices you made, and you wish you never did, relationships you've walked into or out of and you wished you could go back and use a magic brush to paint the picture differently now. When you can accept that where you stand today, or where you have fallen, is the real moment of truth. It is the best gift you can give to your own soul. Forgiveness that doesn't come from the heart is false. It is only scratching a surface level and won't last long,' was how she started.

Prana and Emily avoided eye contact with her, not wanting to be the first one on the guillotine. Jayan and Heidi were less nervous.

'Are you scared to feel true forgiveness?' she asked, softly. 'It's ok if you feel a bit uneasy as today you came with an open heart. This is a good sign. I see a strong willingness to do the work in each of you.'

This put all of them at ease.

Looking at Jayan first, Rose said, 'Did you notice how guilt has become a shadow part of you over the years? It follows you diligently everywhere you go. Your healing is incomplete without forgiveness, both towards others and yourself. With forgiveness, you can get rid of the guilt which has turned into a part of your identity over time. Jayan, do you want to keep living from this shadow guilt or are you ready to claim your power back and live from a higher level of consciousness?'

She turned to Prana next. 'Honey, the same applies to moving on in life from a place of pure joy. If you can step back and observe your situation from a distance, you will notice that you are still holding on to some unnecessary emotions. Can you let go of these peacefully, like soft clouds in a blue sky? Ask yourself, who needs to be forgiven here? You know, good people can make bad choices. And if it happens, bad choices don't make bad people. Have you also thought about self-forgiveness? How much longer will you hold on to the past that's gradually chewing on your peace of mind?'

'Heidi, if you want to find peace in your inner sanctum and carry it with you through life, start with carrying out an inner check. Have you forgiven others? There is a beautiful quote that says, *forgive others not because they deserve forgiveness but because you deserve peace.* Letting go of the beliefs was the first step, and now, what if you could forgive your father and your colleagues for the pain that they've caused you? Today we will create space for the new to manifest.'

Rose shifted her gaze to Emily. 'You've got some work to do before reaching the forgiveness stage as the people involved in your issue are still a part of your day-to-day life and maybe of your future. We need to look a bit deeper into your current situation. A good start would be by observing what gets triggered for you when the others do the work today. Perhaps memories or feelings? Whatever has to happen will come up naturally.'

Today's start was different. After her usual calm meditation start, Rose played Kirtana's *Sweet Streams* song while they were still in the contemplative space. The stimulating words brought them all in a more energetically comfortable space, ready to dive into the sessions.

'We'll do a roleplay exercise keeping the eyes open this time,' explained Rose. 'Jayan and Rose, please move your chairs slightly to face each other. Prana if you will kindly step into the shoes of the person Jayan would like to forgive for the scene we are about to play out. We are in a safe space here, surrounded with the presence of protective angels. Our souls know exactly what needs to happen.'

Glancing at Jayan, she then asked 'Feeling your feet grounded on the floor, your hands on your thighs … and your back resting nicely against the chair… Look into Prana's eyes and relax … Your eyes don't need to strain, they can look into her eyes softly and let your soul be guided …

Who do you see looking back at yourself through her eyes? There is no struggle here … Go back in time … You can take all the time that you need, or it can be as fast as you want … Three… Two… One…'

Jayan took a deep breath and relaxed even more in the chair. He blinked once and his eyes softened a bit more as he replied without hesitation, 'I see my ex-wife Devika here.'

'What would you like to say to Devika today?' asked Rose.

Jayan's eyes glistened with unshed tears. 'I still love you, Devika. I can see with hindsight how my selfish behaviour caused our marriage to fall apart. I am sorry for my lack of communication although you were always by my side. So often, you were telling me about your day, or you tried to have a conversation, but I hardly responded. It's just that I had so much going on in my head and I was already busy planning for my next day. I am to be blamed to a large extent for our marriage not working.'

'If you were to respond as Devika, what would you say?' Rose asked, looking at Prana.

Prana's words came out naturally. 'I tried for years to make our marriage work, but the effort was one sided. It got exhausting and I could not keep on doing this. I felt lonely when you spent so much time at work. You would not even notice the effort I put in the cooking or cleaning. When someone else came in my life, giving me attention and love, I could not help it. You were so busy, that you did not even notice. I am sorry for the pain I caused you.'

'I guess this is what we call taking a relationship for granted. I was focusing on earning the money and I thought that being married meant we would be together forever,' said Jayan with sadness.

'Nothing is to be taken for granted, especially not somebody else's feelings and the effort they are putting to make a marriage work It is two-way. Do you forgive me for leaving?' asked Prana.

Jayan let out a big sigh. 'Yes, I do. It wasn't totally your fault in the first place. I can see my mistake as well, for putting my work before our marriage. Devika, today I set you free from my resentment. I will cherish our good memories for the rest of my life. Please forgive me for all the anger and the bad words I said in the past. I didn't mean them.'

'I totally forgive you. I would probably have had the same first reaction if it had been you leaving me for someone else,' replied Prana.

Rose took over from them. 'Jayan, close your eyes and visualise a peaceful river with a boat tied to a tree. As you approach it, you notice Devika is sitting in the boat. She has been waiting for you to undo this cord of resentment. Are you ready to let her go?'

He nodded. His face softened as he took a couple of minutes to silently say goodbye in his own native language. 'I wish her happiness and watch with a peaceful heart as the boat sails away. I can't remember the last time I genuinely felt happy to see a smile on her face. Today, I can truly say that I set her free.'

Rose asked, 'After recognising that you were also at fault, are you ready to forgive yourself? Forgiveness is incomplete without self-forgiveness. There's a game of self-guilt that takes place behind the stage. Now that Devika has left, check your own being. Do you forgive yourself for the role you played in your marriage falling apart?'

'Before coming here, I thought that I would die feeling miserable, alone and in pain. Over the past week, Lord Ganesh has helped me see that it was my own guilt and anger eating me from inside. Every day a part of me feels clearer now. Somewhere within, there is an inner voice guiding me towards my healing. I can say that I forgive myself.'

'This is very good, Jayan. If you believe in your heart of hearts that you are worthy of forgiveness, then every cell in your body can hear it and is responding. From the top of your head, all the way down to your feet, including the micro cells in your throat are now soaking in forgiveness. Take a moment to notice the transformation,' said Rose.

Jayan replied with a bright smile, 'It's the first time in months that I've been able to talk for so long without feeling this sharp tickling pain in my throat. I feel so much better!'

'You even look ten years younger!' said Emily, making him laugh.

'This is the beauty of being in the moment with forgiveness. It allows us to reclaim ownership of our lives with humility. You can now open your eyes Jayan. Well done,' said Rose.

After a minute of silence, Rose asked, 'Who would like to share next?' Prana seized this opportunity to say, 'I am grateful to be in the presence of wonderful people like you. You have trusted us enough to share such private parts of your lives. I feel more confident now to tell you more about what brought me on my journey to India.'

'The space is now yours Prana,' said Rose.

Their smiles encouraged her to carry on.

'When I found out that I was pregnant, the thought crossed my mind to have an abortion. But I knew straightaway that I couldn't do it. This little one was already a part of me, but there was no way that I could go back to my parent's house in Mauritius, pregnant and unmarried. My boyfriend James and I had only known each other for six months. I was naive enough to hope that he would marry me. I was shocked by his brutal reaction. When I told James that I was four weeks pregnant, he panicked, asked me to leave his apartment, and never come back.'

'Unbelievable,' whispered Emily sadly.

'It is still fresh as if it only happened yesterday. He grabbed my arms and pushed me violently against the wall. He told me to have an abortion, but

I refused. I didn't recognise him anymore. He slapped me and shouted; *It's either an abortion or you leave my life forever.* He went quiet for a moment and added, *in fact, I don't care what you do, just get out of my life! I am leaving for an hour. I want you out of here when I come back!'*

Jayan gasped. 'What an idiot!'

Prana felt a lump in her throat. 'I was in tears as I started packing my suitcase, still trying to figure out where to go or who to call. Then, I found those sleeping tablets in the drawers next to the bed. And I couldn't think straight anymore. It was as if my brain stopped working and despair took over. I feel so ashamed now to admit that I chose the easy way out and, swallowed all of them. I woke up a few hours later in hospital. The nurse told me that James had called an ambulance when he got back and found me on the floor. She said that I was lucky that my baby was still safe.'

Her voice shattered like glass as she dissolved in tears, releasing locked-up grief. 'I felt so worthless. Do any of you know this feeling when you wish you were dead, but you open your eyes, still alive and think why the hell am I still here? What's the point?'

'This was probably your wake-up call. It was not yet your time to go, honey. Prana, you are at the doorway to letting go of what no longer serves you today. Feel James's presence here as you turn and look in Jayan's eyes. What would you like to tell him?' guided Rose.

Prana felt so much anger come up as she imagined James in front of her. 'We could have created a happy family together. You messed up our lives, only thinking about yourself. Why were you so cruel and selfish?'

Rose encouraged Jayan to respond, 'Let the words flow.'

'I was in shock,' he said, honestly.

'You were cruel!' cried Prana.

'Prana, try to put yourself in my place. It was like a bomb had been dropped on me. My reaction was impulsive. I needed more time to digest it,' came the response.

'We could have sat down and talked about it,' said Prana.

'You had already decided that you didn't want an abortion. You are the one who didn't give us time to talk about it. I felt cornered,' responded Jayan. 'After I calmed down, I came back to apologise for hurting you and to talk. But when I saw you on the floor, I got scared and guilty then. I thought it would be a downward spiral if we stayed together. I didn't want to spend my life being emotionally blackmailed by more suicide attempts or God knows what else!'

There was a silence that spoke a thousand words as his reply sunk in for Prana.

'This makes sense but please believe me, I had no intention of blackmailing you. I was scared too,' she said with quivering lips.

Jayan made an expansive shrug with both shoulders and hands. 'Now that the dust has settled, I know you are telling the truth. Neither of us was ready for this, so we reacted in our own ways, maybe with fears from our childhood taking over.'

'I am truly sorry for not handling this situation with more maturity. I thought that you didn't care, and it would probably have been wiser if I had gone for a walk and give you time to think. I can see how I am at fault as well here,' confessed Prana.

Jayan said with softness, 'We all make mistakes. Often, I close my eyes and see again how I mistreated you. I am not proud of my behaviour. Perhaps if I hadn't reacted so violently, things would be different.'

'I am not proud of my actions either. It is still raw as if it all happened yesterday.'

'Maybe we can forgive each other and stop feeling guilty?'

'I'd like this very much. I forgive you James,' replied Prana with a gentle smile.

They spontaneously took each other's hands as a symbol of confirmation.

Rose said, 'Prana, closing your eyes now, I would like you to call upon a mentor with a higher wisdom or God and check with them, what was James' purpose in your life? What was this chapter meant to teach you?'

After a moment Prana answered, 'It was to learn that I am my own teacher, and I can make my own decisions in life instead of believing that I have to lean on others for support.'

'Beautiful words of wisdom. Now that you have understood this and made peace with James, you can say good-bye in your own words. You are in a better place to move on.'

Prana leaned back in her chair. 'Somehow, this feels incomplete.'

'Ok, close your eyes and bring your attention to your body,' guided Rose. 'Visualise the door to your heart opening. Give yourself permission to step into an area of your body that feels incomplete.'

As she relaxed, Prana gradually moved her hands to her stomach. 'Oh, I can feel it is from here … it's my baby! She still feels unwanted.'

'Well done. And now, tune in with her. Put both hands on your stomach, as if you were embracing her.'

Prana was in her own space as she spoke out those words with love. 'You are safe now my baby. I'm sorry for the fear that I caused you on that day when we were taken to hospital. Please forgive me, I was scared. I will not hurt you again. I will always be here to protect you, my beautiful little angel.'

'Perfect … At an energy level, she can sense your love and honesty. She knows that you were lonely and vulnerable back then. Your baby forgives you,' said Rose. 'Allow all forgiveness to take place within you.'

Prana mentioned, 'I can sense it happening energetically. A pink light is embracing us. There's also a hint of guilt left from when my sister died.'

'Are you ready to forgive yourself, knowing that it was the Universe who chose to take your sister away and that you have the right to be here? You have an important decision to make here. Can you forgive yourself? Do you give yourself permission to step into a fresh start with self-love?'

Prana tuned in, to connect with her sister's soul before replying.

'Yes, I forgive myself. I can connect with my sister anytime. My baby is still here. No harm has been done consciously. I can feel something shifting inside me. I feel so much lighter, as if a heavy load has been taken off my shoulders.'

'Lovely! You are creating the space for your own *prana* awakening. I can see the change in your aura. While this is happening, it's very important for you to stay grounded and try the walking meditations in nature,' observed Rose.

'I already enjoy these walks. They bring me so much peace,' said Prana as she opened her eyes and relaxed in her chair.

Rose moved her attention to Heidi, 'How have you been since working on loving your inner child and opening up to the consciousness of Universal love?'

'I've been meditating every day, and I feel a lot of the past guilt and anger have dissolved. I'm in a more positive space. I feel relaxed and sleep better. However, I came here today as I know I still have an issue with forgiveness,' said Heidi.

'You have progressed a lot since you started this journey. You felt hurt many times, but never gave up. Let's check what's going on in your heart today. If you would like to take a nice deep breath in … let it out … and close your eyes,' replied Rose.

'I feel a fire of hope burning in my heart, hope that when I go back to Germany I will lead a happy life, and be able to connect with my family. I love them all so much and I can see how we are running out of time, with my father growing old. But I'm scared that he won't forgive me for choosing a different path from what he was hoping I would become,' admitted Heidi.

'I guess you won't know until you ask him, right?' asked Rose. 'Your father has lived his own life. Place your hand on your heart and ask your heart, who has the permission to justify your life decisions?'

Heidi raised her left hand to her heart, taking a moment to connect with herself. 'This is my choice only. I choose to love my body and soul as I've come to this earth. I give myself full permission to be as I am. And if others cannot accept me as I want to be, this is their choice. And I will not let it affect me,' said Heidi in peace.

'Lovely and this wisdom comes from your higher self. It's your inner truth speaking. Can you still forgive those who might not be ready to accept you?'

'Yes, totally. My love for them is strong enough to encompass anything that requests forgiveness,' she replied.

'In that case, let us go on a journey now and see yourself in one of your favourite places with the people who need your forgiveness. Welcome them and let them know how you feel today at your forgiveness ceremony,' said Rose.

'We are in one of my favourite forests at the crack of dawn. We used to go there for walks on Sundays, after lunch,' explained Heidi. 'Today, I choose to be here just as the sun is rising with the air still fresh and the earth damp under our feet. I can even smell the freshness from the trees around us. This forest is so huge that I brought everyone who has ever hurt me in my life. Family, friends, colleagues, teachers, boyfriends, … they are all standing around. I start digging through the soil with my bare hands. It's so soft that I enjoy the sensation of the dirt going in my nails as I create a space deep enough in the Earth to bury all the pain from my past.'

'Wonderful Heidi, keep going. Pour all the pain from your heart in the deep hole. Let go of anything that you don't need,' encouraged Rose.

'The pain is getting soaked by Mother Earth. I forgive everyone around me. And this space is so magical that they are all welcome to let go of their pain as well here,' replied Heidi.

'What a wonderful thought, go ahead see it happening. When it's all done, you can fill the hole back with soil. Perhaps, even plant a seed in that space now and see what grows out if you visit in the future?' said Rose.

'I love this idea Rose! I can see a special glowing seed in the space now as I fill it up. I will visit the forest regularly to check what it grows into. I am ready to leave,' replied Heidi, before opening her eyes.

'This was beautiful Heidi, well done for listening to your heart. I suggest we take a break. You all had powerful messages today, I suggest and go into silent contemplation for some time,' suggested Rose.

****

Hello James,

I am in a spiritual temple, surrounded with amazing teachers, mountains, a holy river, and all this is helping me to let go of the past. I have made peace and accepted what happened between us. I understand now that it was a powerful test from the Universe.

It feels as though my life has only just started. I am so grateful to be still here.

Today I learnt about the power of forgiveness. It has set me free from harsh feelings both towards you and myself. Neither of us had experienced such fear before and we were feeling vulnerable. I learnt that good people could make bad choices. But bad choices don't make us bad people. A sense of completion comes from being able to forgive ourselves and moving on.

I am grateful for the role that you played in my life. You were a teacher to me. Our relationship was a steppingstone for me to find my life purpose.
I wish you all the best and I hope that you can forgive me too.

Sending peace and light your way,
Prana

She folded the letter neatly and put it in an envelope that she had bought from the small shop at the ashram. Although the forgiveness had already taken place at an energetic level, Prana decided to put it in the post box the next morning. It would be fairer to bring closure for James as well in real life.

****

Emily felt like a thief as she swiftly slipped in the Angel room later that afternoon. She chose a different way back this time, coming from the path at the back of the retreat, to make sure that no one would see her. She was nervous talking about her weight, especially now that some people like Prana and Heidi were friendly. It was easier to blabber in front of strangers who did not care.

She was relieved that Rose had agreed to see her alone. She still felt awkward being the centre of attention when it came to her weight. And she knew it was impossible to just chatter on with Rose. This chit chat game did not work here.

'A penny for your thoughts please,' said Rose, bringing Emily's attention back to the room.

'At times I feel proud of myself and at times guiltier than before. Slightly proud because I eat less. The other day, I was having afternoon tea and I didn't go for a second serving of snacks, which used to be the normal thing before. The temptation wasn't even there. I slowly ate every single piece on my plate, taking the time to enjoy the taste. Previously, I used to greedily devour them so quickly that I hardly noticed the aroma.'

'Very good. What's the guilt about then?' asked Rose.

Emily hesitated. 'The next evening, I found a pack of chocolate cookies in my bag. I thought that there was no harm in having one cookie.'

'And then?' asked Rose, already knowing what was coming.

'I ate the whole pack,' replied Emily sheepishly.

'It must be a tough change for you. Throughout life, both your body and your mind have known comfort eating. It's not only a habit, but also a second nature in your system. Don't expect it to disappear overnight. It works the same way with guilt and shame. They will gradually subside. You need to keep doing the work with your new healthy beliefs and trusting that you are on the right path. Your test is to remain disciplined and persistent in your efforts. Be alert for moments of weakness that will come.'

'It's hard in spite of the new beliefs,' said Emily.

'These beliefs are the first step. I noticed that you haven't worn any makeup since our last session,' said Rose.

Emily blushed happily. 'Indeed, there is no need for hiding myself behind makeup anymore. The new strong beliefs are taking over. It looked wrong when I last tried to paint my face. For the first time, I noticed that it wasn't the real me. I feel more comfortable wearing looser kurtas also.'

'I am pleased to hear this. You look beautiful in them. In order to move forward more comfortably, check with your body, why were you wearing those tight clothes?' asked Rose.

'I felt less fat when I could squeeze into a smaller size. How could I not see until now that these made me look fatter! I'm lucky they didn't burst and reveal my drooping lumps of fat!' said Emily, shaking her head from side to side appallingly.

Rose smiled gently. 'Oh Emily, there's a natural spark of contagious good humour in you. This is your true nature, happiness .... However, honey, right now ... Take a moment, close your eyes. Relax into how you're really feeling NOW. There is no need to make anyone happy. Or even pretend to be happy for somebody else. Be yourself. Connect with the drooping lumps of fat you've been trying to hide for years. They are still a part of you. For now, relax your body and we will do some more clearing today.'

They both rested their backs against their seats and made themselves comfortable.

'Take a few nice deep breaths in and let them out,' guided Rose. 'Visualise the forest you visited before, with tall trees on both sides of a path. As you slowly walk down the path, you get to the area where it splits into two paths leading to opposite directions. There is a bench in the centre, with your *book of life.*'

Rose waited for Emily to nod when she arrived.

'Good ... bring your attention to the neutral area ... with your healthy beliefs, you are now in a stronger position to face the people who made you feel inferior. Invite them for a conversation.'

'There are dozens coming up! My parents, some school friends, and even boys who ridiculed me when I was walking on the road.'

'Everyone is welcome. Pick one person who will act as a representative for the group. Who would it be?' encouraged Rose.

Emily's voice shivered as she said, 'My mum.'

'With your permission, I will act as your mum for this session. Go on Emily, you will only be able to forgive her if you express yourself from the bottom of your heart and let out all the discomfort you ever felt since childhood. Speak those words out now.'

Emily nodded. 'Mum, I know that I disappointed you by not being as good as Amy. I tried my best and it is because I couldn't get there, that I started eating a lot to block the shame. Today, I know that no matter how hard I might have tried, I would never have made it. Because I am Emily, not Amy. I didn't have to walk in her shoes. I am good just as I am. If you think about it, Amy wasn't good at the things that I did well, such as painting and drawing.'

'Painting is a hobby that won't take you far in life. You won't earn as much from a drawing than if you were to be an engineer or a lawyer. I was probably a bit harsh on you, but I did it for your own benefit. I had your future in mind,' responded Rose.

'But mum, what if this was the best for me? There are so many artists who make a good living from what they earn. It doesn't matter if I don't have thousands in the bank like Amy. I want happiness by choosing something I enjoy doing.'

Rose said in a neutral voice, 'A good living might not be enough in the long term when you need to retire.'

Emily was gaining confidence. 'I need to think about what makes me happy in the present moment. I am still young! I don't even know if I will live long enough to retire, and sorry to say this, but by then I will probably have earned money from what dad, and you, would have left. I grew up weak as I considered myself useless. Food made me feel better, but it was like being a drug addict. Once the good effect had subsided, I felt worse and needed more of it. I am still caught in this cycle.'

'I'm truly sorry darling, I didn't know you were feeling this way. You should have told me,' said Rose, acting surprised.

'I was scared to sound foolish. It's partly my fault that I am in this situation today, but I'm determined to change this. I have the power to discover my true potential. I'm learning to eat more consciously and to appreciate my body. I visualise myself wearing a size 10 pink dress and this is what keeps me going. Can you love me for who I am?' said Emily.

'Oh darling, I always loved you. It's just that I find it hard to express my emotions.'

'I guess this is where I got it from then!' said Emily with a sad face.

'We've never been good at sharing how we feel in this family. I have usually expressed my love best by giving gifts, organising parties, or taking the family on holidays. Everyone is not good at providing emotional support, but I'll try to work on this,' came the reply.

'Mum, will you be there for me when I find it hard to resist food temptation?' asked Emily.

'I'm just a phone call away. I can also see you developing your own strength to handle this. You can do it,' replied Rose. 'Please forgive me for not understanding you all this time.'

'I forgive you, Mum. I share the responsibility in what happened by not letting you know how I was feeling and turning to food instead,' said Emily.

Rose stepped out of her roleplay and said, 'See yourself hugging your mum and letting her go ...Good ... Now, with your eyes still closed, imagine yourself looking at a size 10 pink dress behind the window of a retail shop. Are you ready to walk in and try it on, before buying it?'

Emily pulled a funny face. 'What if the size 10 is out of stock?'

'Are you already looking for a reason to doubt that you can lose weight?' asked Rose. 'In that case, imagine yourself standing in front of the window, with only size 14 dresses in the window. It's the only size that you can fit in. How does this make you feel? You can choose to stand there, frustrated, and angry at yourself. Or you can remain calm and walk away, determined to lose weight, and find another shop with size 10 available. Try this exercise by yourself until you get closer to your aim.'

'Good idea! I feel so good that I could run outside naked right now, not bothered about what others think of my body,' said Emily, laughing.

Rose raised an eyebrow, knowing that with Emily anything was possible. 'Hmmm, maybe it's enough to see it happening in your mind's eye.'

'I was joking,' replied Emily.

'Anyway, I would like to check what's been happening with those doubts about Kevin?'

Emily calmed down. 'Our relationship was fine until last month. A close friend pointed out that she noticed I paid for everything. It's true but it never bothered me until that comment. Kevin doesn't work and doesn't try to find a job. I pay for our expenses and often lend him money.'

'Did you have a conversation about it?' inquired Rose.

'Each time I try to talk about it, he gets offended. He says that he truly loves me and that he is waiting until he finds a job to propose to me.'

'Why are you frowning then? I feel you are beating around the bush with the real issue here,' stated Rose.

Big tears started rolling down Emily's cheeks as she spoke. 'I was blown away by his words, until he added that we would only get married once I lose twenty kilos. This scene keeps popping up in my mind during the last satsang meditation. He said it kindly at the time, but now see the sarcasm in his eyes. I don't think Kevin meant a single word. He didn't believe that I would lose weight, that's why he proposed with this condition. How could I not see this? He doesn't love me, does he? He only wants my financial support.'

Rose said with compassion, 'The answer is already within you. Perhaps coming to India, has given you some space and clarity to see this situation with some distance. The truth is revealing itself to you naturally. The time has come to go down the right path in the forest, which you will need to choose. I sense that there is no need for a visualisation this time, Emily as you already know what needs to be done. You may open your eyes.'

Emily looked apprehensive. 'What do you mean, Rose?'

'Take your time for meditation in the temple. When you are ready, have an honest conversation with Kevin. This will be walking down the right path for you. Ask him how he truly feels and see what it triggers in your heart, and how honest the conversation sounds. You have already given yourself the answer here today, when you said what you saw in his eyes. Will you turn the page and have a fresh start on your own? Or will he genuinely ask for forgiveness, and what will you choose then? Be careful that it is not a pattern that comes back in your relationship. You need to meditate on this before calling him.'

'I should probably recite my beliefs a few times before making calling Kevin,' she said nervously.

'Absolutely. Everything will be alright when genuine forgiveness has been expressed in a relationship. If it's not meant to be, you will see the red flags. Your heart is like a cabinet full of resources dear girl. You will know what to do,' Rose contemplated for a moment before asking, 'Do you still paint?'

'At times when I have free weekends,' said Emily.

'Have you considered making it a passion again?'

Emily's eyes lit up. 'I love this idea.'

Once you realize that the road is the goal and that you are always on the road,
not to reach a goal, but to enjoy its beauty and its wisdom,
life ceases to be a task and becomes natural and simple,
in itself an ecstasy.

Nisargadatta Maharaj

Chapter 10

The Awakening at the Ganges

On this fresh morning, they gathered on the shore of the holy Ganges, all dressed in the suggested white kurta sets. Rose had explained that white symbolises purity, peace, and truth in the Indian culture. It would be showing respect to step in the water wearing white. The three-hour shuttle drive was worth every twist and turn of the bumpy journey. Prana could see why the Ganges was so special once they arrived at their chosen part at the foothills. She felt cleansed just by watching the water flow from the Himalayas, clear and inviting. The stunning surrounding peaks took her breath away. She shivered when the cool morning breeze brushed against her bare neck.

'Only ten of you have made it to day twelve of *Finding your Path* retreat. You've learnt about mindfulness and shown resilience towards daily challenges. You broke through emotional barriers and built-up the courage to share about your intimate moments. Take a moment to pat yourself on the shoulder and congratulate yourself for coming this far. If you keep worrying about the future, you miss out on the good work you do,' reflected Aryaji.

They all smiled, and did it, acknowledging the truth behind his words and so grateful to be still a part of the group. Prana was happy that Emily, Jayan, Heidi, and Dev were still here. She could tell that some of them would be friends for life. Nathan looked lost in his thoughts, as he stood behind the master, with his hands behind his back and his head bent.

'You are true seekers now at the doorway of your soul awakening. You have persevered to reach your heart's deepest desire and close to finding your path. It could be so easy, yet why do we find it so hard? That's because we often forget to stay in the present moment. You have learnt this lesson here. Remember, if you stay connected to the light of your soul, it will always be shining on you. Wherever you go in the world, it will be with you.'

Prana wondered for a moment how her life would be when the retreat came to an end. It was impossible to imagine that next week she would be back in England. She would miss the guru's familiar voice. He sounded almost like an old friend now. She strongly believed that perhaps they had known each other in a previous lifetime. She looked past him, at Rose who was meditating on a rock a few metres behind. She would feel an emptiness without her compassionate voice and daily advice.

Aryaji's voice brought her back to the present moment.

'We don't realise how much we can change in a short space of time, until we have to fight for survival with our heads under water. When we stop resisting, we float naturally. Today is your reward for showing determination. Take a full dip in the holy water and let your body rejoice in purity. The Ganges is well-known for cleansing the soul right down to the level of consciousness and setting its visitors free from past karma. Today you have nothing to do. No fighting, no struggling. Allow the sacred water to work its magic until your answers are revealed. Do you have any questions?'

Emily asked solemnly, 'I heard that the water is very cold.'

'At this time of the early morning, it is freezing cold to be more precise,' replied the guru with a hint of hidden laughter in his voice. 'So cold that all your thoughts will freeze to death, even the good ones. It's quite a joyful experience! Let it wash away what you don't need, until Truth is revealed. Stand in silence and listen. Any more question?'

Prana suppressed a smile when Emily glanced at her, in dismay.

Total silence, with the exception of the soft waves.

Aryaji turned to Nathan. 'Nothing, good then. I hand over to you ,' he said, before making his way to join Rose.

Nathan stepped backwards to create some extra space between him and the small group.

'Come on, big smile everyone. We'll start with ten gentle swinging of the arms from side to side to stretch the body. That's it, wonderful ,' he said in a light-hearted voice. 'Now, let's add ten backward and forward moves, shifting the weight of the body from your toes to your heels.'

Prana noticed that he avoided making eye contact with her. '*How strange,*' she thought, remembering how the previous day he had told her that he admired the way she played with Manu. She thought that something had changed in his behaviour, or maybe he was just being professional now, and friendly when off duty.

'I saved the best for today, the *Shakti* shakes. It's a powerful shaking of the body to increase our adrenaline as well as a taster for tomorrow's ceremony. You start by shaking the hands, all the way up to the arms. Then bounce up and down, at your own pace. Now, sweep your shoulders with your hands, imagining all useless weight getting brushed away from your life, once and for all. You don't need this rubbish anymore, get rid of it! Open the mouth slightly to let go of any tension in the jaw. Shake the head from side to side. Keep bouncing while doing this, until you feel out of breath! You can stick your tongue out. It's more fun!' he said, already a bit out of breath himself.

When they all started to puff and pant, Nathan said, 'Lie down, and keep the eyes open. Gently move your hips, feel the pebbles massage your back as you look at the sky… Take a few deep breaths in, expand your tummy like a balloon filled with the fresh air, and let it deflate as you breathe the air out again. Do it a few times at your own pace.'

Nathan gave them a few minutes to feel grounded in their body.

'Turn your senses inside and feel your breath travelling in a straight line through your body. Your chakras might be feeling shy and scared to release their energy fully, after having been closed for so many months or even years. This experience might feel quite new to you. You might want to apologise to them, letting them know that you will now look after them and that it is safe to open up and spread their warmth. You might notice some of your seven chakras getting warmer. Perhaps the root chakra at the base of your spine… or the sacral chakra just above… maybe the stomach… or the heart chakra… or perhaps in the throat area… or the third eye space between the eyebrows. If you are close to enlightenment, it could be the crown chakra at the top of the head… And it's perfectly fine if nothing is happening either. The body has a mind of its own and it will wake up when the time is right.'

'Simply let your body know, it had arrived where it can now rest. The skin on your body will feel the call and you will be guided for your holy dip in the Ganges. When the time is right for you, your own body and soul will work in synchronicity. In your own time, you can make your way to the river. Your feet will know when it's time to take those steps on the soft sand to the holy water,' said Nathan.

Prana felt serene as she stood in front of the scintillating water, with the wet sand tickling her feet, and the sun warming her face. She took a step, in complete surrender. The freezing water was an unexpected shock, especially since her body was still burning hot after all the shaking. Her feet sunk into the gluey sand. The sand settled just above her ankles. She could barely feel her feet which were totally frozen cold. It seemed to take forever to walk up to waist level in the water. The lower half of her body was ice cold by then.

She chose to be brave and dived in. It was sharp pins and needles through her body, as if someone had jolted her with a live wire. She thought that even her brain would freeze from the chill and shock. The pain made her wonder whether it was some sort of a holy payback for lifetimes of sin she might have played on other people. If so, she hoped she had a clean slate and would live *a happily ever after life* from now on.

And then something shifted, like a light bulb had been turned on in the sand that turned hot and bright. Her body could have been an empty bottle literally absorbing the sand that filled it all the way up to her head. She weighed a thousand times heavier, but all that existed was this incredible heat, burning every part of her, until she became the fire. She could not feel her body anymore, but she was aware that she was moving to the pace of the magical waves. Her own wisdom was coming up, a deeper truth from within: *The past has sunk. My future is for me to create as I wish. And so, I shall with absolute joy, excitement and lifeforce.* She was mindful that in this present moment her new power was coming to life. She was not sure how long she stayed in the Ganges, but the sound of people chatting brought her back to reality. Prana slowly made her way back to the stretches of sand and pebbles. She grabbed a towel from the pack that Nathan that kept on the beach and quickly dried herself.

She walked past Mandeep who was lying bare chest on the pebbles, his body shaking slightly. A stranger walking past would have thought that he was feeling cold. However, Prana knew from the euphoric look on his face that it was probably his kundalini awakening experience. A bit further, Heidi was sitting cross-legged, giggling alone with her eyes closed, going through her own experience. She looked around for Emily and saw her lying on her back, with a baby smile on her face and steady breath. She had fallen asleep, looking cute wrapped in a towel. Nathan was still in the water, bowing to the sky with his hands in the namaste position.

She saw another man sitting in a distance. Although his head was bent, she could have sworn from the physiology that it was John, but they had not seen him for four days. She thought he had gone home by now, but maybe not.

Prana sat on a flat rock and made herself comfortable, facing a favorite part of the mountain. She could feel it was speaking to her, so she responded. 'Dearest Himalayas, thank you for giving me the strength to raise my child. I want to be a strong mother,' she said.

'It was always inside you. It is only when you allow your mind to go quiet that you can listen to your own voice,' whispered the mountains.

'How will I know where to go next?' she asked.

'Follow your heart. If you feel unsettled, still wanting to turn left or right, it means you are not yet home. You are at home when you feel at peace,' came the reply.

Everything went quiet. Prana knew it was an indication that was the final answer for now, but today she had created a connection for life with the holy Ganges.

****

Prana left her room at the crack of dawn and headed in the direction of the white marble temple. From the warmth in the air, she could predict it was going to be another hot day. The sunflowers and marigolds greeted her as she strolled past them. She had not been to the temple to meditate on her own again since the cheerful monks scared her away. She was curious to see what thoughts would come up this time. Has she succeeded in breaking the circle of dwelling in the past?

She was surprised to find Emily there, sitting on a bench right in the center. She was looking at the tall amethyst crystal with a peaceful smile. There was no one else around. Prana joined her. The crystal did not make her feel small this time. She closed her eyes and focused on her breath for meditation.

Suddenly, Prana could feel this tingling sensation in her chest and recognised the fear in her body. Her old companion was back when the black hole appeared at the center of her heart. The scary emptiness spread in her arms and legs as the shaking started. She felt small beads of sweat forming on the sides of her forehead. This was all happening too fast for her mind to have time to understand.

'It's ok. You are safe,' whispered Emily.

'The black hole is here,' said Prana, with a shaky voice.

'It's ok. You are safe,' repeated Emily.

The hole kept expanding.

Prana said defiantly, 'I am not going anywhere. You can come and get me this time.'

As soon as the words came out, cracks broke through the wall of darkness. Rays of light came through and started to shine in her heart. Prana was not sure what was happening, but there was no need to understand anything anymore. She just sat there shaking through the fear. Gradually, a massive wave of happiness came from nowhere washing through her whole being. Tears of joy poured down her cheeks as her body did its own thing for a few minutes shaking off the past fear. She gasped in admiration when, in her mind's eye, she saw a being walking through the light towards her. She recognised Durga *ma* radiating in her red outfit with her tiger next to her.

'You are your own strength. All the answers you seek are in your heart. Whenever you need extra energy, I am here for you,' she said.

'Why did you make it so hard for me to find you? Why all this darkness?' asked Prana, quietly in her heart.

The goddess smiled. 'If everything precious in life is given on a golden plate, individuals take it for granted. Your effort to find a reason to live will make you cherish your life and your baby even more.'

Prana asked, 'Am I close to finding my life purpose?'

'You are on the right path, but it splits ahead. You must choose wisely which way to go. Merge with me. I will be here when difficulties come your way,' said the divine voice.

Tears of joy rolled down her cheeks as Prana saw herself shrinking smaller and smaller with each step she took towards the illuminated area in her heart. She embraced her goddess and experienced a transformation in her body. She stayed silent, savoring the newness in her.

'Are you ok?' asked Emily, after a few minutes.

Prana let out a sigh of relief. 'The black hole is gone.'

'Wonderful! I think you might even have been having some sort of awakening,' said Emily.

'Maybe, I felt some heat rising in my spine but too much was going on in my chest. I felt all over the place with the shaking. The energy in the temple is very calming. You reassured me so well, thank you for being here,' said Prana.

'Ah, I've been spending too much time with Rose,' teased Emily, doing a namaste.

They noticed that some monks had arrived for their meditation.

'We should leave before getting told off for talking in here,' said Prana.

The morning get-together was a more relaxed type of satsang. They sat on large cushions in the back garden, waiting impatiently for Aryaji. It was buzzing with intense conversations. Rose and Nathan, who were sitting at the back with their legs stretched out on the grass, glanced at each other. They expected it to be a vibrant get together. They had seen many in the past when the *seekers of truth* gathered after their first visited to the holy Ganges.

The guru joined them and made himself comfortable on a free cushion.

'Namaste dear ones, did you all have a good night sleep? You are all beaming, with eyes shining like diamonds. I think that we won't need a relaxing meditation. Let's dive straight in. Who would like to share about their experience at the Ganges?' he asked.

A few hands went up. He nodded towards Mandeep who had waved both hands, his face glowing with bliss.

'I've been in the Ganges fifty-two times at 20 different locations. Each time before going in, I sat in meditation for hours and put out all sorts of fervent prayers that it would be my day of enlightenment. This time I listened to your advice and thought, *no more expectations.* I simply walked in the sacred river and stood. The divine water that had touched my body so many times felt new to me this time. I knew instantly that it had only touched my ego before. It was the first time I was meeting with the Ganges. I told Mother Ganges, *today I surrender. I let go.* I kept standing there and did nothing else. When old prayers came up in my mind, I let them go like passing clouds. Then, something started to melt inside me. I felt I was sinking in the water and closed my eyes. I couldn't feel my body anymore but knew I was safe. I was getting lighter and floating somewhere new.'

Mandeep closed his eyes in happiness, reminiscing the experience.

'What happened next?' asked Aryaji, bringing him back to the moment.

'For the first time in my life, I then felt this snake waking up at the base of my spine. I could sense it gradually uncoiling and slowly spreading through my chakras all the way up to my head. This brought me such a divine pleasure. I was soaking in a powerful blaze of awakening. This was the moment of enlightenment I had been waiting for all these years. I can still feel this energy in my spine, the snake remained uncoiled and at times I feel like a mad man as I cannot control which way it wants to go.'

He burst out in laughter, with his body shaking as if he was being tickled. They all joined in his contagious happiness.

'You have to be careful,' warned Aryaji. 'You are now your own master and need to guide your energy wisely. Keep meditating and doing yoga to manage your energy.'

'You are the one who showed me the way. Dhanyavad,' replied Mandeep, as he bowed his head in gratitude.

'Now that you have achieved your purpose, what will you do?' asked the master.

'I am not sure. My dream for a long time was to feel the awakening. I stay open to what comes my way now,' replied Mandeep.

'Beautiful. There is immense power in being flexible and allowing the Universe to guide you,' said Aryaji.

They stayed in silence for a few minutes, soaking in the bubbling energy.

Aryaji looked around for the next raised hand. 'Yes, Prana.'

Prana was excited to share. 'My battery is recharged with a fresh desire to live. The black hole has disappeared, and my heart is buoyant with a new love for myself. I have started to appreciate my life as it is. I am grateful for my blessings.'

'Wonderful! You have surrendered to the past and found acceptance! Would you like to tell us more about your blessings?' encouraged the guru.

The words flowed out effortlessly for Prana. 'When I came here, I didn't know what to do with my life. I had taken an overdose a few weeks prior, but I was still alive with my problem unresolved.'

She stood up and placed her hands on her stomach.

'Today, I stand here proud to say that what I thought to be a problem is my sweetest blessing in disguise. I am so thankful to be still healthily pregnant,' she said, her voice radiating with joy.

The others started congratulating her until Aryaji brought their attention back to the gathering.

'There's a vibrant love emanating from you, dear one. I can see how your strength has transformed since you arrived. Now that you see your glass as half full, keep filling it up with positive ideas and more blessings will come your way,' praised Aryaji.

'Every day after meditation, I feel a new part of me is blooming. My life purpose is not yet clear, but I sense that it might be related to children.'

'This is very good. Clarity is slowly coming your way. You might get a better sense of direction in the next session that Rose will be holding,' said Aryaji.

Prana turned to Rose and Nathan. 'I would also like to thank you …'

Her mind went blank.

Nathan had left. She was sure that he had been sitting right there just a moment ago when she raised her hand.

'Thank you for all the support,' she said to Rose, before sitting.

The group's attention was drawn to someone else walking slowly towards them. The man seemed to have aged by ten years with the start of a rough grey beard and bags under the eyes. His dark blue shirt was creased and untucked, adding to his worn-out demeanor.

'It's nice to see you John, please join us,' said Aryaji kindly when the man got within ear-reach.

John sat on a cushion with his head bent and pressed his fingers on his eyelids.

'This is awkward,' was all he said.

'Relax. You are one of us,' said Aryaji.

Mandeep who was sitting behind John, leaned over and touched his shoulder softly, as a sign of confirmation.

John pulled a bunch of grass and fiddled with it. 'On the first day after I left the satsang, I was proud to be walking around without having to talk to anyone. On day two, it started to feel more like it was you walking around, without having to talk to me. I wanted to shout at you, and it was immensely frustrating having to keep it all inside,' he said, still looking down.

'And then what happened?' asked Aryaji.

John swallowed his shame. 'I never felt so out of place. I went for a walk to the mountains for some fresh air, but mostly to get away from where I was clearly the black sheep.'

Aryaji nodded. 'We gravitate towards places that resonate with us. What took place there?'

'The climb was exhausting, and I was out of breath. I found a cave and went inside for a rest. Much to my surprise, Nathan's words came to my mind, and I practiced the *inhale slowly, pause and exhale slowly.* Unlike the first time, it felt relaxing. I started to experience what he called present moment awareness. I felt even lonelier and more miserable, sitting there on my own.'

John looked up, holding back the tears that shone in his eyes.

Aryaji encouraged him with a nod.

'A vision came up in my head. I saw myself as this mountain, strong with an empty cold cave inside. The sun was nowhere to be seen. The sky was hidden behind thick clouds that I attracted like a magnet. It struck me then that it was an illusion to think of myself as an invincible mountain. I wondered, *what's the point of standing strong if I can't control what goes on around me*? I was a prisoner locked in the cold cave of my heart.'

He held his hands up in surrender.

'I spent the whole day and night in the cave. I told it to do what it wanted with me. Memories of past events appeared. I saw how I mistreated people. My ex-girlfriend, who is already rich, had not been after my money. She truly loved me. A prayer came up from nowhere, I begged to be annihilated and reborn. I begged to understand love and feel it. After a while, all thoughts disappeared. Feelings started coming up, mostly shame and inability to trust. After these passed, so much loneliness came up. I just sat there feeling all the times I've been lonely in my life and unable to face it but buried myself in work instead. I lost track of time as I sat in my misery until the sun started to rise. There was a tender warmth growing in my heart. Something had shifted overnight. I don't know what, but I felt reborn.'

Aryaji smiled. 'Dear John, we don't always need to understand everything in our head. You found enlightened awareness by losing yourself in your own presence. You won the battle against your egoic identity. Your new strength is kindness, this is the tender warmth you felt in your heart. Flood your heart with this kindness and your whole being will reside in a warm cocoon of love. There is no point in understanding love and kindness. Simply share it with others. The seed is already growing in your heart. Now you can build bridges instead of walls.'

John said with a shy smile, 'My ego is melting but after dominating throughout my life, it hasn't totally disappeared within such a short space of time. Apologizing for my bad behavior towards all of you feels stuck in my throat. The best I can do for now is to say that I will work on being a kinder version of old self.'

'I appreciate your honesty. The world doesn't change in one day, neither does a person. The time you are taking will make your kindness more consistent. The Universe will test you. Whenever you feel the voice of ego demanding to be heard, treat it like a pair of shoes. Keep it outside the kingdom of your heart. As you progress, there will be no one to wear it. It will disappear.'

'I will remember this,' thanked John.

Emily blew John a flying kiss. 'It doesn't matter if you cannot say the word sorry. I can see the change in your eyes and hear it in your voice already.'

John smiled at her.

****

That same night, they all assembled in the clearing under the greeting light of the full moon. It was watching over them from a sky crowded with a constellation of stars. It looked so nearby that you could almost touch it if you reached out through the trees. They gathered in a circle around the fire with the warm light shining on them. The sound of the crackling dry added a touch of excitement to the scene. They had prepared so eagerly for the traditional *Fire of Freedom* trance ceremony. Four people from the village had joined with drums and rattles. Even Aryaji, Rose, and Nathan who had done it dozens of times, had this anticipation shining in their eyes.

'Lightness exists in relation to darkness. In the same way, *You* exists in relation to *Me*,' said Aryaji. 'We are surrounded by the fire of life, ready to create a more profound connection with the Universe. Ask the Universe for guidance to connect with your own deep-rooted wisdom. Whisper out now for your clarity and path.'

There was a sublime stillness in the energy surrounding them as they all put out their prayers.

'We are here at the energetic doorway to the Universe of the Souls. It is an auspicious night for us to set our souls free. We are one on this spiritual journey. There is no you or me. Our souls will dance together to the rhythm of the music,' he added.

Nathan started beating a *tabla*. His fingers and palms moved in flawless synchrony on the smooth flat surfaces. The drummers and rattle players joined in perfect harmony.

With his eyes closed, Aryaji started moving his body gently to the sound of the rhythm. 'Imagine your body to be like a boat moving freely on the sea of life. Close your eyes now and allow yourself to dance freely to the waves. Let go of what keeps you away from enjoying the dance of life. Strip and pull away the expectations that keep you from navigating your way in life. Move away from the safe banks, take risks until you find new shores. Let go of who you think you are. It's time to dance, shred the old you, and create a new one! When you surrender to the Universe, you can see it has bigger plans for you.'

Prana felt self-conscious at first. She was not a good dancer, but it didn't matter when she saw that she was not the only one. Emily and John were moving slowly, still trying to find their own equilibrium to the music. Jayan looked a bit more comfortable and was already dancing with the flow.

Heidi looked graceful and very natural using a combination of yoga in her dance postures. They each danced in their own way, yet their movements synchronized to the beat of the drums. Rose moved like an angel with her arms raised to the level of her shoulders, her palms facing upwards. She swayed back and forth as if she was dancing with a partner. Nathan was already in the world of nirvana with his head tilted back. His hands moved naturally from one rhythm to another. Prana felt the energy of the sound bubbling through her as he beat the drums faster. Her muscles relaxed as the music got louder. She felt the beats in her heart and her body started doing its own thing. She surrendered to the magic of movement and all state of self-consciousness melted away. She felt so much love pouring in as she kept moving to the music. It was a total state of ecstasy.

'Let your body know your intention to come back to your soul. The time has come for your soul to take over. Your soul wants the very best for you and wants to be wild and natural! Surrender your pains to Mother Nature as you steer back into life with your full lifeforce once more,' shouted Aryaji.

They danced like drunks, laughed like mad and howled like wolves. After a while, they calmed down as the sound of the music slowed down and stopped. They sat around the fire in a calm trance, grateful for this unique experience together.

'Well done seekers,' said Aryaji. 'With this ceremony, your soul has accessed a wider state of consciousness. Let us weave the magic of energy into our body. Look at the stars. They are vessels of energy. Focus on one that you feel most drawn to and invite it to the kingdom of your heart. Imagine a ray of energy flowing from the star to your heart, enlightening it and spreading throughout your body. You have now created a permanent connection between you and the Universe. Whenever your mind feels restless, bring your focus back to your breath. This is the one thing that will never leave you.'

Prana's body was still shaky when she went to bed. Waves of heat rippled through her body, so hot that the mattress seemed on fire. She took her clothes off. She caressed her thighs and moved her hands to the soft area between her legs. It tickled, asking to be pleasured. Prana gently moved her fingers around her feminine spot. It was the first time she had touched herself in this way. She felt guilty for a moment, but then thought that there was nothing wrong in giving herself pleasure. The wetness aroused her even more. She felt the tingling sensation rise through her root chakra and a gust of pleasure explode as she got wet again. The spasms subsided as she bathed in this different sort of consciousness. She was discovering herself in a different way. Life was turning into a beautiful reality.

Everything in the Universe is within you.
Ask all from yourself.

Rumi

Chapter 11

4th Session - The Law of Attraction to Create your destiny

The Angel Room was set up differently each time to accommodate the topic and the number of participants. Five yoga mats with a round pillow on each had been placed in the middle of the room. The wooden table was covered with some drawing pads, colouring pens and pencils, sticker books, scissors, and magazines. Rose stood next to a whiteboard placed on a portable tripod easel. She looked elegant in her long cherry coloured dress. Her hair was tied in a knot, revealing her pearly earrings which matched her ivory bead necklace. She waited them to sit on their mattress before starting.

'It doesn't matter if you aim to be a millionaire, an office worker or a parent, everyone has their own purpose in life. The power to create your destiny lies within you. What's important is to ask yourself, if at the end of the day what you do makes you happy. When you get it right, it will automatically synchronise with the Universe to materialise. It's all about finding the right starting point. You know that you are on track when you feel energised, joyful, and alive doing what you do.'

She asked them, 'What do you want to achieve in life? What are your talents?'

Heidi and Emily shrugged, while Prana and Jayan looked thoughtful. John nervously tapped his pen on the table.

Rose laughed. 'Perfect. I was just making sure that you came to the right place.'

'Where are Dev and Mandeep?' asked Prana.

'They don't need to be here. They are clear about their destiny. Our session today is for those who are still looking for clarity about their path.'

'Mandeep told me that it had always been enlightenment for him. He experienced it many times since we went to the Ganges,' shared John.

'And Dev finds happiness in being a good husband, father, neighbour, and friend. He finds satisfaction in bringing help to others,' said Rose. 'During the night ceremony, he had a vision of himself spreading rainbows of love to bring his community together. His journey to Aruna taught him to open up more and express his emotions.'

'Why is it taking longer for us?' complained Emily.

Rose smiled. 'You are each at different stages of your journey and had your own difficulties to face. It will be easier now that you have cleared some cellular memories and outdated beliefs. In order to attract the destiny that you want, start by writing down everything that is meaningful in your life, what is working perfectly , as well as what is not working at the moment.'

When they each completed their list, Rose drew a circle on the whiteboard and divided it into seven sections: finance, career, relationship, health, spirituality, family, and creativity.

'Draw your circle of destiny and in each section rate the level of satisfaction on a scale of 1 to 10, 1 being unsatisfied and 10 fully satisfied. Now, circle the section towards which you feel most drawn.'

Rose gave the group a few minutes to complete the task, before carrying on, 'What level of satisfaction do you believe you can reach in the section which attracts you most?'

'It is career for me, but rated at only 3,' said Heidi, disappointed.

'I have both spirituality and relationship scored at 6,' said Prana.

'I am pleased but would have hoped for more … 7 in health,' added Jayan.

'I have 5 in creativity but was hoping for a higher score,' shared Emily.

John's sceptical tone was fading. 'I rated finance at 6, but I am surprised as it is already a 10 in my daily life.'

'Okay John, what if you could put away the need to figure it out for now? Take it as a discovery game and treat signs that come up as breadcrumbs on your path,' commented Rose.

John half-smiled. 'It's beginning to sound more interesting.'

'You can all make it a 10 by using the law of attraction. Now that it's been indicated which section on the circle of destiny is more important in your life right now, check what you want to manifest there and why. Prana, it's likely to be a combination for you, so go with the flow and see where it takes you. I'd like you all to lie down, close your eyes, and connect with your destiny vision. There is no time pressure. Your subconscious has the freedom to take as long as it needs. You are merely an observer, allow creation to unfold. The mind doesn't need to take control.'

Rose picked up the antique-looking brass singing bowl that rested on a cushion and gently started to move a wooden stick around the rim. A deep vibrational sound started arising.

'Allow this vibration to help you tune in deeper to your intuitive state where a world of highest possibilities awaits you. As you breathe in, feel the whole of the Universe and destiny breathing in with you. Visualise Mother Earth energy coming all the way from the top of your head, travelling through all your chakras down to your feet, connecting you from heaven and earth. Imagine you are now walking to your favourite place in nature or even a particular place in another country. As you take each step, feel your feet walking slowly, step by step along the path. A sense of familiarity comes up. You've been here before. You've walked down this sacred path of your own destiny. Tune into your heart as you keep going along and invite your higher consciousness. Look ahead, you can see the wonders of your future ahead. It is gently inviting you to your divine destiny. Take your time to see the people you meet and experiences you find on the way.'

The participants embarked on their journey with childlike eagerness and absolute trust. They lay next to each other on their yoga mats, yet worlds apart in their own journeys of imagination as Rose guided them.

By the time they felt fully back in the present moment, Aryaji had joined them for the final part.

'Remember the real reason you came on Earth,' he said. 'Destiny starts off as a seed sown by the Universe. The way it unfolds depends on your thoughts. A whole world is stored in a mind and can be changed by the power of a single thought. Surrender will move you faster than fear ever will. Too often we forget to have fun, play, and relax along the journey. When it all gets a little bit too tense in your mind, just relax. Your destiny will unfold the way it's meant to, so surrender to the greater divine plan.'

'How many of you reached a higher score, or got closer to 10, by the end of your journey?' asked Rose.

They all raised their hands, with different expressions on their face.

Rose turned to Emily who was enthusiastic and, without a shadow of a doubt, finding it hard to sit still.

'Would you like to share first how it was for you, Emily?' she asked.

'It was totally astonishing, although it was not in nature and I was not walking!' she said, bubbling with excitement. 'I started off in a saucer-shaped violet star ship. We flew past funny stars directing us to the landing area. I stepped out right in front of a museum with Romanesque architecture. It was a sunny morning, and the air was filled with happiness as joyful families and couples walked by. I felt instantly at home, walking down the ancient pavement, admiring the work of various painters, watching the entertainers, and listening to the musicians. Portraitists were busy sketching their clients while painters were setting up their easels. And then, I saw it.'

Emily paused to create a moment of suspense. She looked around, making sure that she still had everyone's attention, before carrying on.

'When I saw a vacant wooden seat in front of an easel, I knew straightaway that it was for me. As I got closer, I saw my name carved on it. I sat and started mixing paints on a palette. The second the paintbrush touched the canvas; I knew it was the starting point of my life. The painting came very naturally to me, and I felt a rush of delight inside, like never before,' said Emily in excitement.

'This sounds like a fantastic experience! How certain are you about this?' checked Rose.

'One hundred percent. I was born to be an artist,' asserted Emily with a huge smile.

Heidi whispered, 'I know exactly what you mean. I had a different experience, but which brought a similar sense of confirmation for me.'

'What happened for you?' queried Aryaji.

'I've been stressed my whole life, unaware of it. Stress is a part of so many people's daily lives. We just live through it and get so burnout that it goes unnoticed. It becomes a part of ourselves. If you're not stressed, then it's as though you are not doing enough. You can even be made to feel guilty,' said Heidi.

'That's a strong realisation. What helped you understand this?' asked Aryaji.

'I feel like a new born since this retreat at Aruna. So much has changed in me. I dance, I laugh, and I have fun without feeling guilty! I have been shedding layers of stress and guilt every day. Today, I got a strong message from Afriel that it's never too late to start from scratch. I was taken on a journey where I discovered that my purpose in life is to open a relaxation retreat in Germany. I opened a door and saw myself in a room, holding yoga and meditation classes,' she continued.

Aryaji nodded. 'I can easily see you doing it. How will you achieve it?'

'I received a strong message to join a yoga teacher training school in India and to qualify as an instructor before returning to my country,' said Heidi with glowing eyes. 'This was just the start of my journey. As I walked across the room and opened another door, I saw an expansion to my retreat with a spa, massage rooms and two swimming pools. Doors kept opening in front of me leading to more centres which I will open across Germany. In the last room, I was celebrating with people who came from India to work with me. This will take years to achieve, but if I keep the faith and trust, it is definitely a manageable project.'

'When you believe in your dreams and focus, you can certainly achieve them,' said Aryaji, in satisfaction. 'If you were to rate your career which was at a 3 again, what would it be at now?'

'This is my new career path, to help others find peace and relaxation. It has gone up to 10,' said Heidi, in confidence.

An appreciative silence followed.

'Who would like to share next?' asked Rose.

'I'm blessed to be with all of you,' said Jayan. 'I came here believing that I was doomed to die and with a low energy level. But not only has my health improved to a great extent, I have also found new friends who feel like family, and I have discovered my best friend in myself.'

'You should be so proud of yourself Jayan. You untied the lead ball from your ankle and took a leap of faith. I am certainly proud of you my friend, as I have witnessed your progress here day by day,' said Aryaji with a smile.

'I fight for my life every day with new visualisations and positive affirmations. Forgiving my ex-wife has made me a stronger and kinder person. I can sense the healing happening. The polyps have shrunk, and the pain is milder compared to last week,' said Jayan. The words came out easily, while he could barely speak out a sentence when he arrived ten days ago.

'How did your destiny play out?' asked the guru.

'I saw myself walking down a path to a clearing, and there was a massive movie screen with the story of my life waiting to be played for me. I sat on the grass and watched as it played out. I could see that I came here to support people suffering from similar conditions, by bringing them hope. I will start a charity, by offering them a safe place to visit and talk about their conditions. There will be a phone line for those who are unable to physically travel. I hire volunteers and ask for donations in order to reach more people and expand my charity. I see myself buy a van and go around offering talks. In the movie, I was sitting in a tent, with dozens of people waiting for my first public talk. There were leaflets on a table, with the title *The medicine you seek is you!*'

'Check with your body now, how does it feel in reality?' asked Aryaji.

Jayan sighed. 'Although I am very confident that this is very true and it will all happen, I am not sure how or when. I don't have the money or space to do such an expensive project. I can't even afford a van. And yet it all seemed to be happening, as if everything was already in place. I know it in my heart.'

'That's it Jayan. This deeper knowing in your heart is all that matters. When truth is here, this is all you need to achieve your dreams. The puzzle will fall into place by itself, step by step. Surrender to the journey,' reassured Aryaji.

'Something more came up in my vision. On the screen, I saw a version of myself from the future saying to the present me that I am still work-in-progress. My illness is a passer-by who came to teach me how to grow in resilience and connect with my inner spirit. I'm grateful that the Universe has chosen me as an instrument to help ailing people who have lost hope, discover the power of self-healing and the joy of living again.'

'This is a wise lesson that has come your way. You will be a valuable instrument in the world of healing,' said Aryaji, nodding.

John had been listening to Jayan's journey, mesmerised.

'My direction makes more sense now,' he said, rubbing his chin.

'Would you like to tell us what it was like for you John?' asked Aryaji.

'My finance turned out to be a 6 as I'm not making good use of it. As my journey started, there was a road with a locked gate preventing me from moving forward to the beautiful garden behind. I had to turn back and face all the harm I've done to people with whom I've crossed path in my life. I saw my family, lovers, colleagues, even a shopkeeper and a police officer. An inner part of me stepped into their heart and I felt their pain, all of them at the same time. It was the most atrocious feeling of my life, but I faced it as I did not want to cause people harm again. When the pain passed, I looked at them in the eyes and asked for their forgiveness. It was a wonderful moment; I was able to let go of a heavy weight and darkness. The tall gate unlocked, and I stepped in the garden.'

His face twisted with pain.

'Take your time,' said Aryaji gently.

'A higher being was there, tall and dressed in white. They told me that it was my resurrection day, my chance to move to a higher level and be a better person but that I was not ready yet as there was one person I had not forgiven yet, and it was my own soul. I went down on my knees, brought my hands to my heart, and felt a stem of kindness start to grow right there. The stalk grew deeper as I apologised to myself for all the pain that I had been through during my childhood, and I promised that I would now look after myself and help others in need also. Flowers and trees started growing in the garden around me as I saw myself donating money to charities to help people in need.'

He turned to Jayan. 'Everything fell into place when I heard your experience. Will you allow me to build my first bridge of kindness with you? It would be an honour for me to fund your project.'

Jayan did not expect this. 'Are you serious?'

John smiled. 'You have my word. We can create a voluntary association and set up numerous branches in India. I already have business organisations in England, so I have some experience. This is how my finance destiny rate will up to 10. We can start with one organisation in India and see how it develops?'

'I love this idea! Thank you so much for this opportunity,' said Jayan delighted, as they shook hands.

John looked at Aryaji and said humbly, 'Once our project gets sorted, I'll take a break from my business life and come back to Aruna. I need more help to stay away from my ego and on the right path.'

'You're welcome anytime,' came the reply.

Prana was more than ready for her turn to share.

'Relationship and spirituality merged as the soul of my destiny,' she told them. 'The moment I closed my eyes, I was immediately taken to a garden I visited before. It was where little Manu stays, he was standing in his garden, waiting for me. He pointed towards the village centre, I held his hand in mine, and we walked in that direction. We soon reached an empty building which used to be an old school. As I looked in Manu's hopeful eyes, my path ahead was clear. I know that I want to create a relationship with children, especially the ones with difficulties, by teaching them. I can start with English.'

'This is fascinating,' said Aryaji. 'How does it fit in your circle of life?'

Prana's voice was soft. 'I expected a lot from James. Relationships with children will teach me to love with an open heart. I'll be the lighthouse helping them find their directions in life, without asking for anything in return.'

'I'll progress on my spiritual awakening by focusing more on present moment awareness. With your permission, I would like to carry on coming to the temple for meditation and helping the monks with the gardening meditation. My destiny is in Aruna. My baby's path starts here.'

Aryaji was pleased to hear this. 'The meaning of prana is life force. Perhaps it was part of your journey to find out by yourself that you belong here. Maybe for a short time, or longer. Time doesn't matter anyway. You can start for as long as you wish dear one. You are planning to help the community and good service is always welcome.'

The guru stood up and did a namaste. 'You've all been fantastic, thank you for sharing your journeys. If you stop here and wait for your destiny to manifest automatically, it might take longer than expected. With time, you might even forget your purpose as it recedes at the back of your mind, like an old dream. You must keep visualising it and take actions every day for the law of attraction to work.'

'What if it takes too long and we forget?' queried Heidi.

'The best way is to be grateful as if it has already happened. You own it, so if you express your thankfulness beforehand, an immediate connection is created. There will be tests but absolute trust in the manifestation will attract more from the Universe. If in doubt whether you might have gone sideways from your path, check in your heart. Do you still feel alive and excited?' said Aryaji.

They nodded in agreement.

'Or imagine yourself on your deathbed, and looking back, ask yourself what it is that you wish you'd done, but didn't do?' he added.

He passed on to Rose for the final part of the session.

'We will now give some time to create your mini vision boards,' said Rose, standing up. 'You can draw, use stickers, take images from magazines, whatever feels right for you. It can look funny or serious, so long as the Universe receives a clear signal of what you are seeking. Once the law of attraction starts to work, you are in the flow, and it gets easier to attract your true ideals.'

****

Prana's heart sunk. She had been looking forward to treating herself with a gift after putting in a lot of effort to create her vision board, but the amethyst earrings were gone. A guy had bought them two days ago.

She headed back to the residents' house, wondering where she would live once the session was over. She had to start planning fast. Staring at the colorful flowerpots on the balconies, the thought came up that it might be possible to rent a room here. *'My life will be perfect, surrounded with loving people, positive energy and only a few minutes away from the village.'*

She walked in and noticed a tall man standing in the empty reception area, with a big rucksack and his back turned to her. Maybe he was waiting to meet someone, but there was no one at the desk. It was an unlikely time for a check-in when the course was coming to an end.

As she looked at him leaning in the opposite direction, she had this uneasy feeling in her stomach but couldn't help asking. 'Hello, may I help you in any way?'.

He turned and looked at her with a heart-stopping smile.

A suffocating warmth invaded Prana's chest as her body went rigid in shock. Was it really James? Standing right here in a dark green t-shirt and a pair of brown shorts.

She could see the genuine relief in his blue eyes.

'Oh, my darling! I thought I'd never find you again,' whispered James.

Within seconds he closed the gap between them. Prana trembled as his arms went around her. She had dreamt of this moment countless number of times. Her eyes filled with tears, but she could not bring herself to hug him back. Mixed feelings were coming up.

'I'm so sorry . I made a huge mistake. I went to the hospital to find you, but you'd already left,' said James.
'How did you find me?' she asked, trying to stay grounded.

James kissed her forehead. 'The address of the temple was on the envelope that you sent me. I prayed that you would still be here. Darling, I've come to take you back home. I had so many regrets since this shameful day where I know I reacted badly. Thank you for forgiving me. I always loved you and I want my family with you. I feel more ready now. I will do my best to be the man you deserve.'

'This can't be truly happening…' whispered Prana. She felt hit by a hurricane.
'I know it must be a shock for you to see me, but you can relax. Your life will be easy with me.'
Prana turned her head away. She wished a magic wand would appear and make her vanish in a puff. James frowned. 'What's wrong, honey? You wrote that you have forgiven me.'
She closed her agitated eyes.
'I thought you would be happy to see me,' said James in apprehension.
'I'm just a bit … overwhelmed. So many things have changed in the past week. James, I feel my path is here now,' she replied.
'What about our baby? Our baby deserves a family life also.'

Prana heard alarm bells ringing in her head. 'It feels as if you are trying to decide my life for me James. I don't like the sound of this. I am able to make my own decisions. And I have feelings for you , but more importantly, I have also learnt to love myself now and I will not tolerate having people in my life who do not know how to show me respect. This is a lot to take in right now.'
'Okay, maybe I'm being a bit too fast. We have an important decision to make about our future. I will stay in the town centre and come back to talk about it tomorrow,' said James, as he stepped back.
He kissed her gently on the lips before leaving.
The sweetness of his kiss brought back a rush of bittersweet memories for Prana.
'What if he's right? What if we're meant to be together? How do I find out if James is my true path …?'

****

Prana was about to knock on Rose's door when something within stopped her.
Instead, she turned around and walked briskly to the temple. With every step, she could feel her determination building up.

'Arjan ji, Nathan and Rose have taught me everything I need to know. I can be my own teacher and I now have all the resources to handle this situation on my own. The Universe is with me.' She sat cross-legged on the marble bench and stared boldly at the tall amethyst crystal in the centre of the room.

'Whoever is playing this bad joke on me, we need to talk,' she whispered firmly.

She was confused when a vision of Durga *ma* appeared. Calmly, Prana asked her, 'Why are you doing this to me?'

'The time has come for you to build up on your strength. Stop going left and right to look for answers and advice. Stay centred my girl, and you will find that your path is right here,' came the reply.

Prana wanted to hear more. This was not enough. She knew the next reply would come if she tuned in more into the silence. She focused on her breath and the voice came back.

Durga *ma* said, 'You have to walk the walk on your own for some time. Stop looking for emotional support in the wrong place. You have been asking for it from people who don't have it themselves to offer it. Once you realise how strong you are on your own, the right people will come in your life naturally. The Universe is now offering you a choice between two paths. If you're given the only option of staying here, you will always keep thinking how it would have been with James. The Universe is offering you a choice. The ball is in your court. Make a wise choice, my girl.'

The deity's image faded and was replaced with a straight path. She could see an image of James holding her hand. They were wearing their wedding rings. She saw their love growing over the years they lived together in London. Their two children joined them in the walk. At first, she would miss Aruna and often think about her moments of truth and the people she had met there. It slowly faded into the background, leaving a trail of emptiness and she'd feel a pinch of sorrow when a sudden memory would come up. Her family was her life but no matter how much love there was in their lives, this emptiness was anchored deep down in her heart of hearts. Aruna had taught her who she truly was.

She took a deep breath and brought her attention back to the present moment. Another image came up. This time she was standing with her feet soaked in the water of the Ganges River. She felt more serene, but lonely. It started off with a sense of emptiness which gradually filled with elation as her relationship with herself, and her daughter, grew stronger. She didn't have a partner, but gradually felt complete in every possible way, surrounded with divine Universal love. Her spiritual process progressed slowly and turned into a mind-blowing awakening, with her body and soul dancing in pure joy. She felt a presence behind her. She stepped out of the holy water and saw a silhouette in the distance. It was somewhat indistinct, and she struggled to recognize the man, but the blue eyes looked vaguely familiar. She had seen them many times before. She trusted his energy and felt safe as he got closer. Before she had time to recognize him, the vision smudged away.

She remembered the words, *Imagine yourself on your deathbed…*
In her mind's eye, Prana lay there, ready to let go of her physical journey. Her heart filled with regret when James showed up. As their relationship grew stronger, the one with herself died. She never got to find out who she truly was. Her destiny became nothing but a false fairytale to please him. Her lighthouse switched off and she never saw the children she could have helped on their own journeys.

Prana opened her eyes with immense relief.
It was now crystal clear in her mind what she needed to do.

Somebody I loved once gave me a box full of darkness.
It took me years to understand that this, too, was a gift.

Pema Chödrön

Chapter 12

The Beauty and Pain of Love Satsang

The two girls got to the satsang room, early as usual to secure their seats in the first row. It was beautifully decorated with extra candles lit for this last evening together. Vases of fresh flowers brought an exquisite scent to the room.

'Are you sure about your decision?' asked Emily, with a hint of concern in her voice as they sat down.

She had seen Prana say goodbye to James earlier in the garden. She had not meant to spy on them but stayed around in case her friend needed help. It seemed to be an intense conversation at first, but Prana had looked calm.

Prana nodded. 'Although I had many doubts about what to do, when my mind came at peace with the past crisis, I was able to see through the whole situation a lot better. My heart found the answers and I knew that James was a closed chapter in my life. As we talked through it, even he admitted that my refusal to return to London with him brought him some relief. He was trying to do what feels right, but deep inside he is not ready to take full responsibility for being a father or handling a family yet. We'll keep in touch. My new book of life has started, and I hold the pen.'

'Has someone else taken his place?' asked curious Emily.

Prana gave her a strange look, 'Maybe…'

Emily almost jumped out of her chair. 'I knew it! Is there something going on between Nathan and you?'

Prana shook her head. 'I enjoy Nathan's company very much, but right now I need the time to discover and appreciate the journey with my own soul. I am still learning to nurture myself.'

Prana was grateful when the others started to turn up and interrupted their conversation. As much as she was fond of Emily, she was not ready to share about her emotions which she was still exploring. Much to her surprise, Rose sat next to her instead of choosing her usual cushion on the floor.

'I left my teacher's outfit in the bedroom today,' she joked.

Before Prana had any chance to reply, the satsang had started.

Aryaji cleared his throat. 'Welcome dear ones. Well done to those of you who made it to day 10 of the retreat. Love has always been one of my favourite themes … that's why I saved the best for our last gathering. What is love? It's like a double-edged sword. It can bring you so much happiness … or pain. You have the option to choose on which side to be. Or it's like a fence, you can sit in the middle and feel nothing, until you accidentally fall on one side. And it might be a surprise on which side the wind blows you. I would like to have your thoughts on love.'

'It can be hard work, especially for someone like me who has not experienced profound love. I would choose to sit on the fence and wait to see in which direction of the fence the wind blows,' shared Heidi.

'Don't worry, as self-love develops, the door to your heart will open and make it easier for you to find the love you've been seeking,' he replied.

'Yes, I feel more open and prepared for a relationship now,' said Heidi with a smile.

'What about those whose heart have been stabbed by this sword of love? I am done with love. I've experienced it, felt the pain. I would not want to go through this again,' asked Jayan.

'You can keep twisting the sword in your heart or pull it out and let the old bruise heal. You don't know what will grow once healing has happened. Allow space and time for something fresh to emerge,' said the guru.

'Very well master,' said Jayan.

Emily felt brave and was happy to share today. 'I called my boyfriend Kevin yesterday, or after the discussion we had, I should now say my ex-boyfriend. I can see that I was with him for all the wrong reasons. The love was one-sided, only coming from me. I was also seeking some sort of validation from him, which I don't need anymore. Listening to him on the phone, his words did not sound authentic. I could see how we were not truly connecting at the heart level. He was more like a leech hanging on to me for money and comfort. I will not settle for anything less than respect, love, and honesty now. I made the decision to let go of him, there and then!'

'Emily, you are radiating! You have released a part that was not serving you. Well done for realising this! How did you feel after this?' praised Arja ji.

'I thought I would be miserable as I loved Kevin so much. But in fact, I felt good riddance, and a tiny bit of sadness,' replied Emily.

'This will open a better future for you. You deserve better than someone who was taking advantage of you. Be patient, give yourself time to heal. Always listen to your heart first,' was the advice.

Aryaji tilted his head back and moved his gaze to the door. He signaled to Nathan, who was standing at the doorstep, to join him on the couch. Nathan could not hide his sadness as he sat in front of everyone. His armour of perfection had fallen.

Aryaji touched his shoulder. 'I can sense today's topic might be a good one for you, my friend. We are all in this together. Would you like to share what is bothering you?'

Nathan shook his head with disappointment. 'Guruji, I was in full control of my destiny and my emotions. My sword of love was standing straight on the fence. I was determined to become a yoga master, but I feel like the Universe has played a bad trick on me and I lost all control.'

'Let's take it one step at a time. First, you need to forget that you are a yoga teacher. You are also a human being. Good. Now, relax and go back to that specific moment when you lost control. What happened?' asked the guru.

Nathan's eyes were filled with sorrow. 'I was extremely upset by something I heard a few days earlier. I felt a sharp pain in my heart, which came as a shock to my system. This shattered the emotional stability that I put so much effort to assemble. I didn't need much reflection to realise that I had fallen in love. This changes my whole perspective about my journey to become a spiritual master. And I don't think this person will reciprocate my feelings as they are on their own journey.'

'Can you welcome this as an amazing experience or test that has come your way to explore? What if you could give up the need to figure out how it will all end up? As time goes by, you will see that there is so much left to love in this world and so little time. Love it all as it comes to you. Maybe this is a sign that you are not meant to fight your emotions, welcome all of them, as they come. Even if at first it is a fire that burns right through your heart. Through it all, you will feel this deep love becomes stronger and transforms into unconditional love,' reflected Aryaji.

'I wanted to be like you master, emotionally strong and driven by unconditional love. You look at everyone with the same love in your eyes. But I fell in love with one person and lost my bearing,' admitted Nathan.

Aryaji laughed. 'Relax, Nathan. You don't have to stay single in life to focus on your spiritual path. It was my personal choice to have spirituality as my life partner, but I could have been doing the same thing while being in a relationship. The key is to let go of your need to control this love.'

'I don't know how, there are too many questions in my mind. This love controls me already,' replied Nathan.

'You've heard this quote dozens of times. *If you love someone set them free. If they come back, they're yours. If they don't, they never were.* But I say, even if they come back, they aren't yours. Nobody belongs to anybody. This is called attachment which might lead to other forms of unhealthy emotions such as jealousy, fear, resentment. Unconditional love brings happiness,' replied the guru.

Nathan's voice was choked with emotion. 'How do I get rid of this heavy pain in my chest?'

'Welcome it as a new friend who wants the best for you and is knocking on your door to take you a step ahead on your journey. Sit with it, walk with it, sleep with it, eat with it, feel it … do whatever you need but stop fighting it. Let it bring you down to your knees and then see what happens,' said Aryaji, firmly.

'How will I know when I pass the test?' asked Nathan.

'Your spiritual progress has been consistent over the years but be careful not to be so tenacious that you can't see the wood for the trees. The Universe sent you an earth angel to shake your grounding. Maybe the message here is that if you get too rooted in your mission, you might forget the beauty around. Don't try to control every step in your life. You are fulfilled already. Take it one step at a time. Give yourself permission to enjoy life, while still being vigilant. There is no need to know right now about the signs of success in the future, you have it all in you already Nathan and you will know when the time comes. One sign will be when you can look in the other person's eyes without feeling any pain, not even the size of a grain of sand ,' advised Aryaji.

'Thank you, master. With your permission, I will leave now, and take some time to meditate on your advice. I need to take some time to plant my feet back on earth and practise finding myself again,' said Nathan.

There was an awkward silence hanging in the air after he left.

Aryaji spoke slowly. 'Ok everyone, we will all learn about self-remembrance, but first let's talk about this information Nathan has left us in the room. Satsang is meant for truth sharing so all emotions are welcome here. We all probably guessed that he was talking about Prana.'

Prana had not expected those words to be spoken out loud. She blushed with guilt as she could sense the others looking at her.

Aryaji reassured her. 'Prana, let go of the guilt that I can see on your face. We are in people's lives for a reason, a season, or a lifetime. All of you have played a role in each other's life during this retreat. There's a reason why your paths have crossed here.'

Prana let out a sigh of relief. 'I enjoy being with Nathan but there is too much going on for me at the moment. I need time to love myself, I still need to figure out what it means to become a mother and consider where I will be living.'

'Absolutely. Just take it one step at a time. Love has its own way to flow like an effortless river if it's meant to be,' said Aryaji.

He looked at everyone in the room. 'For now, close your eyes and we will do a short exercise. The moment you seek love outside, you try to find validation from somewhere else. You always have this sense that something is missing, you live with a sense of loss, and you seek it from somebody else. I know you want to be loved and seen. But, what if you could be still? When you chose to be here, instead of always running after love… always seeking from somewhere else… something starts to relax within. You break the cycle. Stillness takes over. Your own heart opens up. You find out that you can give yourself what you need. There is no need to run around anymore as you start to remember your lost parts. You can give yourself what you have been seeking for from elsewhere dear beloved. You need to take a moment and pause in life, to remember all this love that already belongs to you.'

Aryaji paused for a sip of water. 'At some point today, I would like you all to do a short exercise in your own time. Find a tree in the gardens and hug it with all your love. As you stand there, imagine you are hugging a present-day version of yourself and let it know, or say those words out loud *I love you.* As you hug your tree, place your attention in your heart space. Let it know how you have been running after love your whole life, but you've had enough of this now. You were brought up with beliefs about how you are a half so that you seek your other half from the world. Your heart is ready to receive what it desires now. You know that you are already whole. You don't need somebody to complete you, but someone with whom you can share your fullness. Someone to stand next to you in richness, depth, and love. Follow your heart. It will always lead you to unconditional love. Place your attention on your breath. Your heart is your home. It is beating in a steady rhythm with all your life joys. You can always bring your attention here when you need advice. If you trust in your heart, it will guide you to the right choice.'

****

As the two of them made their way back to the hostel, Rose said, 'It will all be fine. The Universe has a way of making things fall in place smoothly.'

Prana took this as the right moment to ask something that had been on her mind.

'When we had Satsang at the Ganges, and you were meditating on the rock, I saw you look in our direction a few times.'

'That's normal,' replied Rose, perplexed about this remark.

Prana hoped that she was not walking on eggshells with her comment. 'What I mean is, you were actually looking at one person in particular, with so much love in your eyes.'

Rose gave her an amused look. 'If you are trying to ask me whether I love him, some questions are better left unanswered. The answers you are looking for are in the unspoken words, in the eyes, in the respect shown for each other, in that which could have happened but never happened between him and I. Let's say that Aruna temple will always be the second home to my heart.'

Prana thought carefully before asking. 'Does Aryaji know how much Aruna temple means to you?'

'The master knows everything, even if we don't talk about it in detail,' said Rose.

'But why not?' insisted Prana.

Rose smiled, 'You heard what the master said earlier. He has chosen his spiritual path as his life journey. I knew this from the start, but as you heard, love is not something that can be controlled. He is my teacher for unconditional love.'

Prana paused about the concept of love as they walked along the path, how it could all be so easy or complicated. 'Rose, are you happy?'

'Absolutely, what I have in my life this is plenty. Most importantly, I enjoy what I do, I feel balanced and healthy. My heart is filled with infinite happiness,' confirmed Rose.

Prana did not think she was ready for this sort of unconditional love relationship. She still wanted to experience a relationship with a partner, but simply needed some time to learn to love herself first, before being ready to embrace someone else on her journey.

There was a small package with a note waiting for her at reception. She opened the package first and was stunned when she saw the same pair of pear-shaped amethyst earrings that she had hoped to buy from the shop. Her hands were shaking as she unfolded the note. It was not signed, but there was no need for that. She recognised Nathan's handwriting from the notes he used to leave in the yoga classes.

Namaste dear Prana,

I am leaving Aruna temple today as I set off to meditate at a different temple for a few weeks or months, until I learn how to love unconditionally. I don't know if we will meet again. Please don't try to meet me before I leave, I don't think I can talk right now, I need to find my grounding first. If it's meant to be, our paths will cross again.

Although the news was a shock to me at first, I want you to know that I love you as you are, with your baby, lovely earth angel. I also respect that you need your space, and I will not be in your way.

Look after yourself.
Nathan.

Epilogue

7 months later

Over time, Prana discovered that Aruna had a language of its own. She felt supported in every way by the magical temple. She could not have dreamt of a better place to bring her baby into the world. She pulled Mindra closer to her chest and kissed her forehead.

'You are my precious gift,' she whispered, as Mindra gave her the most heart-melting gurgle.

Prana felt blessed as she looked around at the guests who had come for Mindra's welcome ceremony. She was so glad that Rose was able to coordinate her trip with another upcoming retreat. After the celebration in the Angel Room, they brought their stools close together and looked like a small family, busy catching up. Aryaji listened to them like a delighted father who was seeing his children after a long time.

John and Jayan explained about the new charity centre RosArya that they opened in Delhi, with three branches across India. Jayan was totally healed and held regular workshops on positive thinking. Prana had listened to some of his motivating radio shows. Dev glowed with happiness as he proudly shared news of his new job as the town mayor. He was interacted more easily with people since his stay at Aruna temple. Heidi could not make it, as she was busy managing her yoga centre. She was also working on a project for the spa construction.

Aryaji told them that Mandeep passed away the previous month. 'A monk found him lying peacefully in one of the caves in the mountain. He spent a lot of time in meditation, and I am sure that he is with us in spirit.'

Prana smiled in approval when she looked at Emily. They had kept in touch after she returned to Malaysia and were now close friends. Emily had lost weight, stuck to her ambitions and was busy shaping her art career. Her paintings sold at well-known exhibitions. She had met a man, and although it was still early days in their relationship, things looked promising.

John interrupted her thoughts. 'How's it going at the school?'

Prana beamed. 'I'm so glad that I went ahead with this project! The monks here kindly helped me with the renovation work and the school room was ready a month after our Law of Attraction session. Two of them are helping me with the teaching classes. We have fifteen pupils from the neighbourhood. And thank you for contributing to the running expenses.'

'My pleasure,' replied John.

Nathan reached out to take Mindra from her arms. 'Your arms are probably screaming for some rest now,' he said.

'You're just looking for an excuse to take my doll away,' replied Prana as she kissed him on the cheek.

Jayan seized this moment to ask them. 'Is there anything that you forgot to tell us?'

'Not really,' replied Prana, blushing.

'But you never kissed me,' said Jayan, pretending to look upset.

'Nor me,' added Dev and John.

Nathan laughed. 'I've worked hard to earn this kiss! When I returned to Aruna after three months, I've been around helping her throughout her pregnancy.'

'Hmmm, I'm not convinced,' said Jayan.

Emily shrugged. 'Don't bother, I tried many times. You won't get a straightforward answer from either of them.'

Prana glanced at Nathan and they both suppressed a smiled as the others carried on with the banter. Prana was still unsure where her feelings would lead to and preferred to take it slowly.

And she was fine with not knowing.

Affirmations & Meditations

I can do it!

I deserve the very highest and best

I am perfect just as I am

I am pure joy

Happiness is my right

I am enough

This too shall pass

I am healed in every possible way

I stand in my own power

I am my own teacher

Peace is my right

I totally love and accept myself

I am the creator of my destiny

I trust the Universe will manifest the highest and best for me

The Crystal Meditation

Start by putting out an intention.

It can be anything that you might want to change in your life, a dream you want to manifest, improving your health … or it can be something as simple as staying happy.

Pick up a crystal

Feel the weight of the crystal in your hands. Feel the shape.

Feel the energetic connection between the warmth of your hands and the coolness of the crystal.

Feel the warmth and the coolness merging and becoming one.

Visualise a bright light emerging from the crystal and spreading around your hands.

Allow it to become bigger and brighter.

Imagine it surrounding you. It is now protecting your energetic space.

Ask if it has a message for you.

Thank the crystal.

The String of Energy Meditation

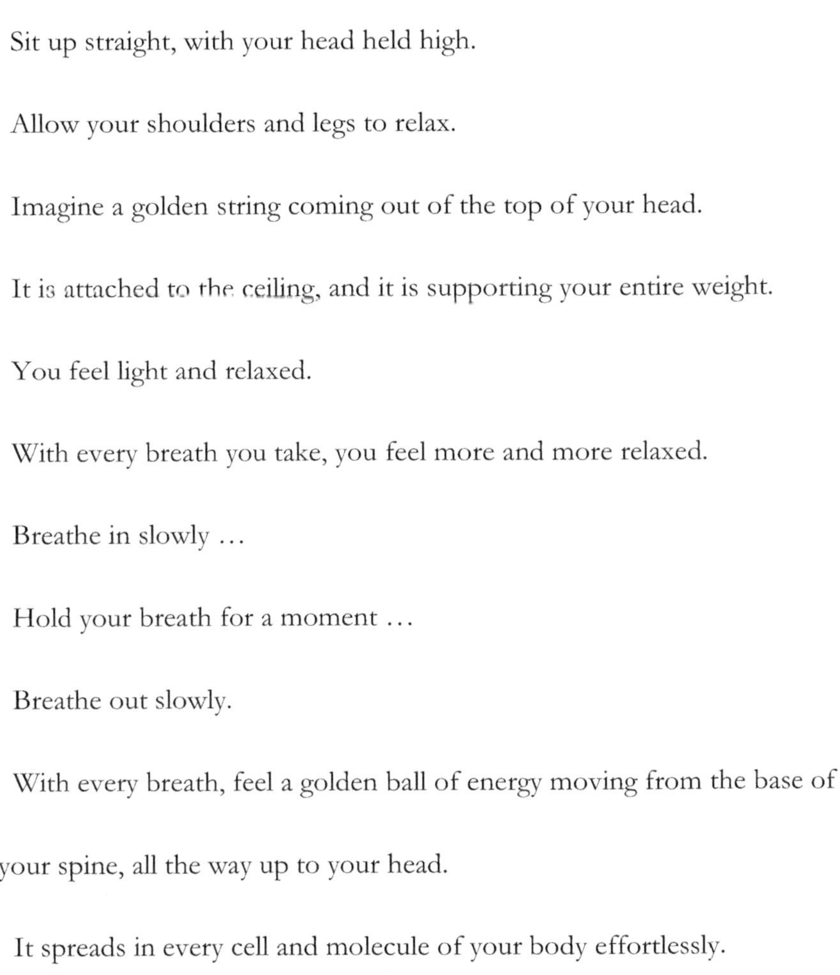

Sit up straight, with your head held high.

Allow your shoulders and legs to relax.

Imagine a golden string coming out of the top of your head.

It is attached to the ceiling, and it is supporting your entire weight.

You feel light and relaxed.

With every breath you take, you feel more and more relaxed.

Breathe in slowly …

Hold your breath for a moment …

Breathe out slowly.

With every breath, feel a golden ball of energy moving from the base of your spine, all the way up to your head.

It spreads in every cell and molecule of your body effortlessly.

The Loving Kindness Meditation

The original name of this practice is ***metta bhavana***, which comes from the Pali language. *Metta* means 'love' (in a non-romantic sense), friendliness, or kindness: hence 'loving-kindness' for short. It is an emotion, something you feel in your heart. *Bhavana* means development or cultivation.

In the first stage, you feel metta for yourself. You start by becoming aware of yourself, and focusing on feelings of peace, calm, and tranquillity. Then you let these grow in to feelings of strength and confidence, and then develop into love within your heart. You can use an image, like golden light flooding your body, or a phrase such as 'may I be well and happy', which you can repeat to yourself. These are ways of stimulating the feeling of metta for yourself.

In the second stage think of a good friend. Bring them to mind as vividly as you can and think of their good qualities. Feel your connection with your friend, and your liking for them, and encourage these to grow by repeating 'may they be well; may they be happy' quietly to yourself. You can also use an image, such as shining light from your heart into theirs. You can use these techniques — a phrase or an image — in the next two stages as well.

Then think of someone you do not particularly like or dislike. Your feelings are 'neutral'. This may be someone you do not know well but see around. You reflect on their humanity and include them in your feelings of metta.

Then think of someone you actually dislike — an "enemy", traditionally— someone you are having difficulty with. Trying not to get caught up in any feelings of hatred, think of them positively and send your metta to them as well.

In the final stage, first of all you think of all four people together — yourself, the friend, the neutral person, and the enemy. Then extend your feelings further — to everyone around you, to everyone in your neighbourhood, in your town, your country, and so on throughout the world. Have a sense of waves of loving-kindness spreading from your heart to everyone, to all beings everywhere. Then gradually relax out of meditation and bring the practice to an end.

(From https://thebuddhistcentre.com)

For holding back, the light you gave to me
For every feeling I denied
For all the hurt I could have turned to tears,
But turned inside.

For every heart I could not open to
And all the dreams I never dared.
For every time I turned my back on truth
When I was scared.
I forgive myself. I forgive myself.

Sweet streams wash me down
Pour your grace over me
Lift me up to a higher ground
Where I can see.

For blaming you when life got hard to live
For all the joy I could not see
For everyone whom I could not forgive
Or let go free.
I forgive myself. I forgive myself.

Sweet streams wash me down
Pour your grace over me
Lift me up to a higher ground
Where I can see.

Now I know what I've been told
That you've been right here looking out for me
With a shower of blessings that you had to withhold
I'm not going to fight it anymore – let it be.

Sweet Stream lyrics
Kirtana

Glossary

Masala	a mixture of ground Indian spices
Hindi	an Indic language of northern India
Rani	queen
Aap kuch khayenge	will you eat something
Mujhe maaf karo	forgive me
Mein khana bechta houn	I sell food
Dhanyavad	thank you
Kundalini	female energy believed to lie coiled at the base of the spine
Guruji	spiritual teacher
Gopi	female cowherd
Satsang	spiritual gathering
Namaste	respectful greeting
Tarka dahl	a dish of creamy lentils cooked with onion, garlic, and spices.
Thali	a stainless-steel platter
Surya Namaskars	sun salutation postures
Mala	a string of beads used for meditation
Sukriya	thank you
Pan	medicinal betel leaves containing sesame seeds, dry coconut kernel, fennel seeds, cloves, dried fruits.
Moksha	release from the cycle of rebirth
Tabla	music instrument made of two barrel-shaped drums
Shakti	cosmic energy

Acknowledgements

With Gratitude

I would like to thank those who stood by me, believed I could do it and kept their trust in me.

I begin with Brandon Bays and The Journey work. Her powerful and regular online Satsangs always point me in the right direction with the right words at the right time.

Thank you to Lan Taylor-Tran, Ramesh Ramdoyal and Iain Spooner for your encouraging words and support when reading the manuscript.

With gratitude to my loving father Ashok and my dear sister Ksh who are forever by my side in their formless presence.

Thank you to my dearest mother Vijaya, all family and friends from Mauritius, UK and spread around the world, especially to Lan, Vero and Krity who were there for me on the phone.

I would like to thank Bournemouth University for offering me the job, and my colleagues for their support when I was going through a transition phase in my life.

www.journeyhealing.net

07545 983998

Printed in Great Britain
by Amazon

10386301R00098